Turn Back Time

Turn Back Time

Pamela Fudge

ROBERT HALE · LONDON

ISBN 978-0-7090-9844-7

Robert Hale Limited
Clerkenwell House
Clerkenwell Green
London EC1R 0HT

www.halebooks.com

Typeset in 11½/17pt New Century Schoolbook
by Derek Doyle & Associates, Shaw Heath
Printed in Great Britain by the MPG Books Group, Bodmin and King's Lynn

If we are all judged by the company we keep then I must be doing something right, because I have the best friends in the world. This book is dedicated especially to Pam W who shares so many coincidences with me including a passion for puddings and poetry, and to Jan and Chris N who have shared forty years of laughter and tears with me, but mostly laughter it has to be said – often hysterical. Also to fellow writers, like Chris H, Nora, Lyndsay, Alan, Bruna, Cass and Janie, and those I relax with, including Karen, Nicky, Sally, Robert M and Robert B. I'm so lucky to have you all in my life.

CHAPTER ONE

The front door slammed and my daughter wandered into the kitchen as casually as if she'd just come back from the corner shop and not from a fortnight in the Dominican Republic with her father and his latest girlfriend. She dumped a bulging holdall in front of the washing machine and then turned her attention to me.

'Hi, Mum.' She dropped a kiss on the top of my head and moved straight on to the stove to see what was cooking for supper.

'Meggie, lovely to have you home.' I'd looked up eagerly from the neat hem I was stitching the minute I heard the key in the door, but my tone was equally casual. 'Good time?'

'Mmmmm.' She nodded. 'Brilliant,' and then nodded again with evident approval as she checked the contents of the oven. 'Shepherd's pie, Mum, my favourite and made just the way I like it with lots of cheese on top. You're a star. That's nice,' she continued, indicating the material I was working on.

'It is pretty, isn't it?'

Already heading towards the door again, she asked over her shoulder, 'How long until we eat? Only I really need a shower first.' Indicating the strategically placed bag, she added, 'Afraid I brought quite a lot of washing back, along with a bit of a tan. I hope you don't mind – about the washing I mean, not the tan, because I think it suits me.'

She was laughing as she reached the door. I was smiling, too, as I resumed stitching.

'Oh,' she stopped, with her hand casually resting on the side of the door, 'Dad said to tell you he'd like to have a word.' Then she was gone and I was left staring down at the needle I had just thrust deep into my finger and at the crimson stain already marring the delicate cream fabric I'd been working on.

Even as I was fetching a plaster and working to remove the blood before it ruined the material, questions were running round my mind like a pet hamster in one of those exercise wheels.

'Have a word.' What on earth did that mean? I hadn't had 'a word' with my ex-husband that wasn't absolutely necessary since our acrimonious split when Megan had been little more than a baby. In the early days we had endeavoured to put on some kind of front for the young Megan but, as she grew up, any personal contact between us had became rarer than hen's teeth. What was it that suddenly needed to be said that couldn't be dealt with by text or email in the usual way? That was what I wanted to know.

It obviously had to be something to do with our daughter, since she was our only link, and I immediately started to cast about in my mind for whatever it might be.

If it were anyone but Megan I would have come up with some of the more worrying teenage scenarios, such as drugs, pregnancy, STDs, but she had the level head at eighteen that both her parents had unfortunately still lacked even at a greater age.

She'd had the same boyfriend for four years – and he was as sensible as she was. Both had sailed through GCSEs and A levels and come out at the end with the necessary subjects and UCAS tariff points to ensure places at their universities of choice. Single-minded in the pursuit of their chosen careers, they appeared to accept with equanimity the separation they would inevitably face when they attended different universities. Tom's future as a vet and Megan's as a midwife had never seemed less than a certainty to me.

By the time Megan came back down, wrapped in her favourite towelling bathrobe and with her damp hair falling in auburn ringlets to her shoulders, I had put the sewing away and the washing machine was whirling round as busily as my thoughts.

Over heaped plates of steaming food I dared to ask the question, 'So did your Dad say what he wanted to talk to me about?' in a carefully disinterested tone.

With her mouth full and giving the plate in front of her her full attention, Megan shrugged. 'No.'

What, not even a hint? I wanted to say, and to press for a lot more detail than that one unsatisfactory word, to insist that he must have said *something*, but old habits died hard and I was too used to leaving Megan out of any dealings I'd ever had with Chay. He had also been careful to do the same, which made it all the more unusual that he had sent a message to me via our daughter on this occasion.

'I think he's going to phone you and suggest a meeting,' she offered as an afterthought, before ladling another generous helping of the shepherd's pie on to her plate and tucking in with gusto.

Well, it was ridiculous to let the thought of speaking to Chay make me so jittery that I jumped every time the phone rang and, as the evening progressed, I got more and more cross with myself and more and more angry with him. If the thought of a simple phone call was doing this to me, I dreaded to think what meeting him in person was going to do for my equilibrium.

Just what the hell did he think he was playing at, suddenly deciding he had to speak to me after all this time? The time for any kind of a reasonable conversation to take place between us was long over. I couldn't think of a single thing he might have to say that I would want to hear.

Megan had taken herself off to spend the evening with Tom, and I'd already answered three calls – each time with great trepidation – all of them turning out to be queries regarding my dressmaking services, when the phone rang again. Predictably, I almost leapt out of my skin and, convinced that this time it really was Chay, I was horrified to see that my hand was actually shaking when I reached out to pick up the receiver.

'Hello,' I snapped, rather more sharply than was polite.

'Oh, dear, I'd better call back another time when you're in a better mood. Who's upset you, or aren't I allowed to ask?' My mother's soft laugh tinkled down the line and I felt my own mouth curve in response.

'You don't want to know, believe me,' I told her.

'Do you want to try me?'

'No,' I said, but then it tumbled out anyway. No one else knew how badly it had ended between Chay and me, so no one else would understand my concerns as well as my mother would.

She was silent for several moments and the line hummed between us. Then she said, 'Perhaps Charles is thinking of getting married again and he wants to tell you first, or ask you to help him break it to Meggie. You did say he had a girlfriend, didn't you?'

Relief rushed through me, followed swiftly by another feeling I couldn't quite identify, and I laughed. 'Now why didn't I think of that? Though why we have to meet up to talk about it is beyond me. He could easily have just sent me an email.'

'For goodness' sake, Tessa.' My mother sounded unusually impatient with me. 'You were married to the man for several years, you've been divorced now for at least fifteen, and yet you still can't bring yourself to be

11

civil to him. Charles isn't a monster, he didn't murder anyone. Marriages fail all the time, and I'm sure there's no need for this continued animosity. It's very unhealthy to hold on to anger, you know. Have you never heard of water under the bridge?'

'Well,' I said, trying not to sound as offended as I felt, 'that's me told.'

'You always insist you have no feelings left for the man, so why you can't even allow yourself to be in the same room as him after all this time is beyond me.' She was beginning to sound more exasperated by the minute. 'He's little more than a stranger to you now, after all. What harm can it do to meet Charles, listen to what he has to say, and behave like the mature and reasonable woman that I know you are?'

She was right, of course. My mother didn't often offer advice or even an opinion, but when she did she spoke the best common sense of anybody I knew, bar none.

'How did you get to be so wise?' I asked ruefully.

'It takes years of experience,' she said and changed the subject adroitly, knowing she had made her point.

I was calmer when I came off the phone, but still jittery about taking the expected call, and cross that Chay could still affect me like that after all these years. In the end I decided I wasn't just going to sit around waiting and did what I always did in times of crisis: I hid myself away upstairs in my sewing room. Cutting, pinning and machining pieces of fabric together forced me to focus on the matter in hand, until my mind was clear enough for me to consider sleep.

Tessa's Togs. I smoothed the familiar label stitched into a finished garment. Not very original, but it was the best I had been able to come up with, and my own creations, together with a steady flow of alterations and repairs, had given me a reasonable income over the years and total independence. Being self-employed had also allowed me to fit my working hours around Megan and her needs. I counted myself lucky to be able to earn a good living doing something that I loved.

Megan came and put her head around the door when she came home. 'Still up?' she asked. 'You must be working on something important because it's getting quite late.'

I could have said I was working on my own insecurities, but I didn't think she would understand, and how would I explain the trepidation I felt at the mere thought of meeting again, after so long, the father she loved so dearly.

'I was just about to pack up,' I said, realizing that Chay was unlikely to ring at that time of night, and I started tidying things away. 'Do you want some hot chocolate?'

'I'll make it,' she offered, and tripped off down the stairs.

By the time I got down there the drinks were made in our special mum and daughter mugs and Megan had found the bourbon biscuits I kept in for her. I watched her dunk one for so long that I expected it to fall with a splash into the steaming chocolate. I was amazed when it reached her mouth in one piece.

She closed her eyes, apparently savouring the soggy

offering, then, opening them again, she said, 'It's nice to be home, Mum. I shall miss times like this when I go to uni.'

'So will I,' I told her with feeling, but refrained from asking again why she hadn't chosen the local university, or at least one closer to home. I reminded myself, as I had before, that she was growing up and naturally wanted to spread her wings.

'And I'll miss Tom.' She looked glum for a moment, and then added cheerfully, 'but it's not for ever and there are the holidays to look forward to.'

Not for the first time I wondered where she got her common-sense approach to life from. It was impossible not to remember that when Chay and I had faced similar choices we had decided, clearly without a lot of thought, on reflection, that we couldn't be without each other for a single minute. That had been our first mistake. It had been the first of many.

In the end, after I'd had an uneasy night's sleep, the phone call came when I wasn't even inside the house to take it. Pleased to be getting some early September sun after a fairly miserable August, I was making the most of its rays by pegging out Megan's holiday washing to dry, and I didn't even hear the phone ring. Caught up in household chores, it was some time before I noticed the green light flashing and, impatient to get back to my real work, I pressed the button to retrieve the message without giving a thought to whom it might be from.

To say I was shocked to hear Chay's voice was an understatement. I sagged against the hall table, gripping the edge until my knuckles went white, so distracted by the disturbingly familiar tone that I didn't actually hear a word he said and had to play the message over again.

'Oh, Hi, Tess – erm – Tessa, I hope you don't mind me ringing. Something has come up that I really need to discuss with you and I don't think it's something that should be dealt with over the phone.' Chay sounded every bit as uncomfortable as I felt in listening to him. He cleared his throat noisily and continued, 'I've taken the liberty of booking a table at Annabelle's for eight o'clock on Friday. I thought it would be more civilized to talk over a meal. I will pick you up at quarter to. Please text me if that's agreeable to you.'

I was stunned and ended up in my sewing room machining seams furiously while I fought the very desperate urge to text an abrupt message telling Chay to go to hell. When I had calmed down sufficiently I sent a terse text agreeing to meet him. It had to be something important, I reasoned when I could eventually manage to be even a tiny bit rational, for him to want to arrange a face-to-face meeting. I was quite sure he couldn't seriously want to see me any more than I wanted to see him.

It definitely wouldn't be anything to do with us personally, I decided without a second thought; our relationship had been over for years. That left only Megan as our one remaining link. It must be something to do with her, and something significant enough to make it imperative that we should meet up – after years of avoiding each other like the plague – to discuss it.

What information did Chay have about Megan that I wasn't privy to? I couldn't even begin to imagine and in the end I made an effort not to try, which was all but impossible. Neither was it easy to stop myself from asking Megan prying questions that might give me a clue about what was going on in her life that was giving her father such great concern.

I wasn't sure whether to share with her the fact that Chay and I had been in contact and that we were actually meeting each other that week. She appeared to have forgotten about the message she had passed on to me, so when she shared the fact that she would be spending the entire weekend at Tom's parents' it seemed easier just to say nothing.

'You can spend some quality time with Martin,' she suggested brightly, which was generous of her, since she had to make a real effort to hide her dislike of the latest in an embarrassingly scant selection of the Mr Not-quite-right-but-OK-for-now men who had been part of my life at one time or another.

'Mmm,' I muttered noncommittally.

Megan wasn't to know that I'd had to cancel a date with Martin to accommodate the meeting with her father, and I saw no point in mentioning it. To say he hadn't been pleased was a massive understatement.

'What's so important that you suddenly have to meet again after – how long is it?' His tone had been icy.

'Around fifteen or sixteen years,' I said obligingly, adding, 'and I don't know what's so important, which is

16

why I've agreed to our meeting.'

'Sixteen years,' he repeated, 'and then he clicks his fingers and you go running.'

'Hardly. It sounded important and probably concerns Megan, so I will be going.' I didn't add, *whether you like it or not*, but the unspoken words hung between us. As did the rejoinder that he expected me to go running when he clicked his fingers and that – to my shame – I usually did.

'I see.'

It was clear that he didn't and he hung up in the end quite huffily, without making arrangements to meet another time. I found that I didn't really care very much at all and was quite surprised by that, since I was always reminding myself what a catch he was.

Megan left at lunchtime on Friday and I immediately began to fuss over my appearance and what I was going to wear that evening – at the same time also despising myself for giving a damn. However, I defy any woman worth her salt not to want to look her best when meeting up with an ex, even if he was one she wouldn't touch again with the proverbial bargepole.

I should have had my hair cut, it was certainly long overdue and looking quite messy. I fingered the over-long bob despondently and even wondered for a brief moment whether I could possibly book myself in for a quick trim. Reminding myself that Fridays were the busiest day of the week at the salon that I preferred to use put a stop to that line of thought. I washed my hair instead, drenching it in Megan's super new conditioner, which, from the

17

claims on the label, promised to magic away my split ends.

With a towel around my head I turned my attention to my wardrobe which, given my talent for dressmaking, should have been full to bursting with originals. The opposite was in fact true. I was a bit like the builder whose own house was falling down through lack of attention. I grudged paying out for quality high street fashions, but rarely had the time or inclination to spend making garments that would update my own image.

When at last I left the house, I felt reasonably pleased with my appearance. My auburn hair hung straight and glossy to my shoulders, and I was dressed conservatively in a black dress that was my own creation and was little more than a shift that fell in tiers to my knees. This had the effect of giving me a smooth outline, with any imperfections well hidden, and showed off my slim legs, clad in glossy black tights, to perfection.

I had insisted on meeting Chay at the restaurant, feeling I could easily cope while there was a table between us, but perhaps not so well in the close and more intimate confines of a car. The evening was fine and dry and still reasonably warm, and the restaurant wasn't that far away, so the decision to walk there was an easy one. It gave me time to calm myself right down until I felt totally in control of myself, and of my emotions. By the time I got there I had as good as convinced myself that Chay was little more to me than a complete stranger and that that was how I would treat him.

That conviction lasted until the moment I stepped into

the restaurant. My eyes met Chay's straight across the room, and I felt the years roll back. I had to get another good grip on my emotions before I stepped forward with a slight smile on my face.

It was so unfair: he hadn't changed much at all, though there was grey in his brown hair that wasn't apparent until I got closer. He could still generate that deceptively open smile to order, I observed rather sourly, but I was pleased to note that there were lines around his dark eyes that used not to be there. However, it didn't look as if he'd put an ounce of weight on over the years and I found myself breathing in self-consciously.

He rushed to pull my chair out, beating the waiter to it. 'Tessa,' he said formally, 'thank you so much for coming.'

We ordered drinks and studied the menu. I didn't care what I ate and told him to order for both of us, which he did, and then we looked at each other across the table.

'So, Charlie.' I couldn't quite bring myself to call him Chay, the name for him that had always been for my use only. I thought Charles would have sounded ridiculous, given the fact that we had once been husband and wife. 'What's all this about?'

'Well.' He paused, then rushed on, 'I don't quite know how to say this. . . .'

'Well, I suggest you *try*,' I encouraged him with emphasis.

'I think we might still be married,' he said abruptly.

CHAPTER TWO

Still married.

Those last two words seemed to reverberate around the packed restaurant and I was amazed that nobody else appeared to hear them.

Unfortunately, I had been taking a sip of wine as Chay began to speak. The shocking statement turned the sip into a gulp that immediately went the wrong way. I choked and gasped for air, bringing Chay to his feet and the waiter running.

'Is madam all right?' the waiter asked anxiously, as Chay pounded my back with rather more vigour than was strictly necessary, though it did the trick and air trickled again into my labouring lungs.

Mopping streaming eyes, I managed to say hoarsely, 'I'm fine now, really. I'm fine.'

'And the wine is acceptable?' the waiter persisted.

'There is nothing wrong with the wine,' I insisted, 'or me. It just went down the wrong way.'

All too conscious of how red in the face I must be and wondering how much of my mascara had run, I just wished they would both stop staring at me.

'Perhaps some water,' I suggested, giving the waiter something to do. The minute he had scurried off, and Chay had sat down again, I demanded, 'What the hell do you mean, still married? We can't be. I distinctly remember divorcing you – I had a solicitor and everything. I have the decree at home.'

The waiter returned with the water jug at that point, jingling with ice cubes and flavoured with lemon slices. He made a great show of pouring me a glass and watching as I sipped it.

'Lovely,' I assured him, willing him to go away. 'That's much better. Thank you so much.'

Finally satisfied, he left.

'Decree nisi *and* decree absolute?' Chay was staring at me a little too closely.

I didn't like to show my ignorance and ask what the difference was. I'd had little to do with divorce – apart from my own. Most of my friends over the years had been sensible enough to remain single, and those who'd married had managed to stay that way. Anyway, as I had already pointed out, I'd had a legal representative to do whatever was necessary to end my and Chay's marriage with very little input from me.

'Of course,' I said with a conviction that I was suddenly

21

far from feeling. After all, it was a very long time ago and I'd had no reason or inclination to revisit information from a time that had been very painful for me.

'Oh, that's good.' Chay sounded so relieved that I felt kind of offended that he was so transparently pleased to know he was rid of me – even though I knew that that was plainly ridiculous. We'd been living separate lives for years.

The waiter arrived back with our starters at that moment and I stared down at the deep-fried mushrooms that had once been a great favourite of mine. I was ridiculously touched that Chay had remembered after all this time, and then was really cross with myself for even caring that he had, and purposely pushed them around the plate instead of just tucking in, despite the fact I was still particularly fond of them.

'Are you planning on getting married again, then?' I asked in a careless tone of voice. A thought suddenly struck me. 'You're not already married, are you?'

'Of course not.' Chay sounded affronted. 'I wouldn't do that without telling Megan – and you,' he added, in an afterthought kind of way that I found vaguely insulting. 'I may be taking the plunge again in the near future, though, which is why I'm asking you about the decree absolute.'

The waiter appeared again right on cue, and looked concerned at the number of mushrooms on my plate that quite clearly hadn't been touched. I assured him it was me and not the mushrooms that were to blame, and tried

vainly to ignore a mouth that watered with regret as he
took them away.

'Congratulations.' I was pleased with my hearty tone,
and voiced surprise that he had waited so long. 'According
to Megan you've been an item with what's-her-name for
some time.'

'Does she like Millicent, do you know?'

'That's something you would have to ask Megan. She's
old enough now to speak for herself, you know.'

'Yes, of course. Sorry.'

The main course arrived with all the rigmarole that the
placing of plates and dishes involved. The waiter looked
at me with such concern that I knew I would have at least
to try and do justice to a lamb shank that looked
absolutely enormous. Too late now to say that I rarely ate
red meat any more when Megan – who loved it – wasn't
around, I thought ruefully. I had no one to blame but
myself for leaving the selection to Chay.

I helped myself to a minuscule amount of the creamy
mashed potato and added similar portions of carrots,
cauliflower and broccoli and wondered how I was going to
get any of it down, despite the fact I was actually really
hungry. Then I had to watch with some envy as Chay
loaded his plate with gay abandon. Sitting across the
table from his ex-wife obviously wasn't affecting *his*
appetite, I realized, and I wondered what was the matter
with me.

'So,' Chay chewed a mouthful with obvious enjoyment, swallowed and continued, 'you have the decree

absolute, then?'

'Of course, as I've already said.'

'That's good. Only when I contacted the court they didn't seem to think it had been applied for by either of us.'

'Really?' I tried to ignore the feeling of deep unease that I immediately experienced, and gave my full attention to getting some of the lamb from the bone and on to my fork. 'That's ridiculous, because it's something my solicitor would have dealt with, surely?'

'Just what I told them, and they've said that if I can provide a copy it will make it easier to trace. I expect they get cock-ups like this all the time.'

'Yes,' I agreed.

'So, you'll let me have a copy, then?'

'Yes, I've said so, haven't I?' I said touchily, knowing full well that I had said no such thing. 'I'll give it to Megan,' I added quickly, just in case he suggested meeting again, then I swiftly changed the subject to talking about people we had both known at school and what they might be doing now.

By the time we'd finished the main course we were chatting quite easily and between us had managed to fill in most of the gaps, particularly regarding those who had shared various classrooms and teachers with us through most of secondary school. The only slightly depressing thing was the realization that some of the other couples who had paired up during school as we had, had lasted the distance and were still together.

I was amazed when I realized all that was left on my plate was a bone, much to the waiter's very obvious delight, and I was happy by that time to be persuaded to order a sweet from the delicious choices on offer. Somewhere along the way I had stopped feeling self-conscious in my ex-husband's company and stopped worrying that by some mischance we could still be married, because that was clearly ridiculous and not even worth contemplating.

At the end of what had been a surprisingly pleasant evening, I refused a lift in Chay's four-by-four and walked home, alone with my thoughts. Part of me was tempted to start looking for the decree absolute the minute I stepped through my front door. I successfully fought the urge and enjoyed a cup of tea and a couple of Megan's bourbon biscuits – which went down very well, despite the fact I'd already eaten more than I normally would – before going to bed, where I slept soundly until well after my usual time.

A good part of the day was spent planting spring bulbs, before I went indoors to put the finishing touches to a rather glamorous creation for one of my favourite customers. I wasn't much of a gardener but did like to see the brightness of daffodils after what always seemed like a very long winter and I liked to plant early, before the weather got too cold and damp. The dress I was working on was destined to be worn cruising on the *Oriana*, no less, when the wearer would be celebrating her birthday. I looked forward to seeing her pleasure when she saw the finished garment.

It was early evening before I gave a thought to digging out the paperwork that Chay had asked for. Being self-employed I was a stickler for keeping receipts, invoices, bills and anything of an official nature for probably far longer than was necessary. In fact, if I was being truthful, I kept absolutely everything of even minor importance for ever, just in case, so I had no doubts about finding this particular document with relative ease.

A search of the filing cabinet in the corner of my sewing room came up with nothing of any relevance, but that was hardly a surprise, given that anything kept there tended to be of a current nature. This meant a trip up into the loft was necessary and a rummage around the boxes of old files kept up there.

With a deep sigh and great reluctance I collected the pole I needed to lower the hatch, went out on to the landing and in no time had retrieved the ladder and climbed up into the boarded space above. A ghostly kind of place, it was lit only by a single bulb that cast long shadows from the rails of clothes hanging there and full of things that 'might come in handy one day'. I navigated my way past suitcases, old pictures and framed photos to a pile of boxes stacked in one corner.

It had been a long time, and I might have known the paperwork would be in a box at the back of the pile and at the bottom of the box, but eventually I held a folder retrieved from a number of identical folders, each labelled with the contents. This one was labelled *Divorce Papers*. I didn't read the letters, just flicked through until I came to a document with an official stamp on it and breathed a huge sigh of relief as I drew it from the folder and almost gave in to the urge to laugh hysterically.

I was still smiling as my eyes scanned a printed page giving our names, the name of the district judge and the date of the court sitting. Following this was the date and place of our marriage, but it was the statement following this that made my heart sink all the way down to my slippers.

There, in black and white, was the declaration that the marriage *has broken down irretrievably* and decreed that *the said marriage be dissolved unless cause be shown to the Court within six weeks from the making of this decree why such decree should not be made absolute.*

No, that wasn't right, it couldn't be. I carried the paper across to study it underneath the light but the wording hadn't miraculously changed. There was nothing about the decree being made final and absolute; in fact when I looked more closely it clearly stated in bold print: **This is not the final decree**.

I rushed back to retrieve the folder and the rest of its contents, whacking my shin on the corner of a picture frame in my haste. I returned to sit under the light bulb and sifted carefully, examining each piece of paper until the print was blurring. I felt sick with growing unease when I realized that I had no memory of ever receiving the crucial decree absolute. I was becoming more certain by the minute that the paper wasn't merely mislaid but had never been provided. No wonder the court had been unable to find any record that the marriage had finally and absolutely been dissolved.

I soon discovered it's no easy thing to think back to a time so long ago, but I intended to give it my best shot as I climbed down out of the loft, pushed the ladder back in place and secured the hatch. I even brought the paperwork with me in the vain hope that I was mistaken and that the document had been there all along.

Sitting with a cup of tea among the mess of papers spread across my kitchen table, I was forced to be honest with myself. The decree absolute was conspicuous by its absence and had either been thrown away in error, ripped up and destroyed by me in a fit of fury, or – and this was the most likely possibility – it really had never been sent to me in the first place. I was as certain as I could be that I had never applied for it myself; quite sure that it was something I would have remembered.

In my heart I knew the decree hadn't been thrown away; I was far too careful for that, and however angry and upset I had been at the time, I wasn't foolish enough to have destroyed a vital document in a fit of pique.

I took a sip of the rapidly cooling tea and rubbed the bruise on my shin thoughtfully. The more I thought the more convinced I became that I had never been in possession of a decree absolute. The question then was, was this due to an oversight on my part? Had I been instructed to apply for the decree or was that the solicitor's job? I eventually matched the decree nisi with the letter it had come with, which said very little apart from pointing out that the decree nisi was enclosed.

The question was, where did I go from here? To the solicitor's office was the easy answer, but at 9.30 on a Saturday night I was unlikely to find anyone working there. However, it seemed easier to do something rather than nothing. I stood up, picked up my car keys and reached for the letter to remind me of the address, though I found I remembered fairly clearly where the office was once I put my mind to it. I suppose certain circumstances keep some places clear in your mind even many years later.

The sky was dark as I drove across town and a misty rain had started to fall. By this time memories were starting to stir and I could clearly picture the large old house with the solicitors' name board outside. Amberswell, Whitburn & Misserbell. The recollection of the name-board always reminded me of how miserable I felt every time I kept an appointment that would bring the end of my youthful marriage closer.

I had felt like such a failure and was probably a total mess. It was just as well I had never seen any of the partners because a very nice clerk had done his patient best to deal with my paperwork, my tears and me. I wished I could recall his name.

I turned the corner into a wide street and took the slip road on to a service road that was immediately familiar, lined as it was with very large houses that in those far off days had all been occupied by various companies offering professional services. Probably they still were. Number 82 looked exactly the same as I remembered and I breathed a sigh of relief.

It was in darkness, as I'd expected, but at least it was still there and I could return on Monday and sort this whole mess out. As I stepped out of the car for a closer look I was already picturing how we would smile over such an oversight, and maybe even laugh about how I hadn't even noticed that I didn't have the most important document from the divorce process of over fifteen years ago, until now.

It was raining quite hard, and I don't know what made me walk right up to the house, instead of just jumping back into the warmth of the car. The board, still in the same place, was partly obscured by straggly shrubs that were in need of serious pruning, but when I was close enough to read it through the rain and the leaves, my heart almost stopped beating as I read, **The Brankstone Medical Centre**. Following this was a list of named medical staff.

'No-o-o-o.'

I found myself running up and down the road, reading the signs for dental practices, beauty salons, and any number of law firms except the one I was hoping to find.

I looked up and down the tree-lined road, and in the distance caught sight of a lone man walking his dog. He was obviously local to the area and might have some information. I waited for him to get close enough to talk to, cursing both the dog and the number of trees delaying the man's progress.

'Excuse me.'

He stopped and stared at me, looking very wet and quite cross. His Alsatian just strained towards the next tree in line and ignored me totally.

'Can I help you?'

'Sorry, you must be eager to get home out of the rain,' I apologized, 'but I wondered if you knew what happened to Amberswell, Whitburn and Misserbell, the solicitors that used to be there.' I pointed to the medical centre. 'Have they moved to new premises?'

He moved close enough for me to decide that he was quite elderly. Late seventies, maybe even early eighties. He looked like a man with important information to impart.

'Ah, now,' he said, 'that was a strange case. I remember it well, though it was years ago – about fifteen is a fairly accurate guess. Some sort of scandal – to do with elderly clients' money, I always reckoned – all hushed up, though. They were here one day and gone the next as I recall. It was as if they'd disappeared off the face of the earth.'

'Oh, I see,' I said faintly. 'Thank you very much. Enjoy the rest of your walk.'

I climbed into the car and sat for a long moment staring out into the darkness and pouring rain, wondering how on earth I was going to tell Chay that it looked as if he was right. We very probably were still married.

CHAPTER THREE

Sunday morning, far too early, found me wide awake and with my fingers itching to pick up the phone and talk to someone – anyone. After a sleepless night, I was fed up to the back teeth with worrying alone about the dilemma of the missing decree absolute. It was a toss-up whether to share this concern with my mother or with the other person whose name was on the original divorce petition – Charles – bloody – Wallis. The man whom I had happily been assuming all these years was my ex-husband.

Yes, actually, why not him? Why should I be the only one to fret about this? If I hadn't given a thought to the lack of a decree absolute – well, neither had he. Had he applied for his copy sooner he would have been aware long before this that there didn't appear to be one, realized that there was a problem and been able to alert me.

While I was right up there on my high horse I reached for the phone and pressed for the number that was programmed into the memory for Megan's ease of use.

'Megan?' A deep and very sleepy voice answered and the knowledge that I had obviously woken Chay gave me a selfish kind of satisfaction. 'Do you know what time it is?'

'It's not Megan, and yes, Charlie, I do know what time it is.'

'Tess-a.' I heard the rustle as he sat up in bed and I wondered fleetingly whether he was alone. He sounded suddenly wide-awake as he asked, 'What is it? A problem? Something to do with Megan?'

'A problem?' I repeated. 'Well, yes, I think there might be. Nothing to do with Megan, more to do with us and the matter we discussed on Friday night.'

I could almost hear the cogs turning over as his brain processed this information. I waited for the clang when the penny would eventually drop.

'We're still married?' He sounded horrified.

'We might be,' I admitted, and added sarcastically, 'and you don't have to sound so delighted at the prospect. I don't want to find myself still married to you, either.'

'I'll come over,' he said. The line went dead before I could tell him that we could sort this out over the phone and his coming to my house absolutely wasn't necessary.

I'd been up for hours and had followed my usual routine regardless of my concern over the missing paperwork, so I knew I was looking a lot less rough round the edges than Chay did when I opened the door to him. I took a lot of satisfaction from that.

Dressed in a rumpled navy sweater and jeans that looked as if they'd been picked up either from the floor or out of the laundry basket, Chay wore loafers on his feet but didn't appear to be wearing any socks. His dark hair stood on end and he was unshaven. I, on the other hand, was wearing a clean white T-shirt, skinny jeans and strappy sandals. My hair was freshly washed and straightened and I'd even applied touches of lipstick and mascara. Not that my appearance mattered, of course, but I did feel the fact that I looked ready for anything gave me a certain advantage.

'Come in,' I said to thin air, because he had already marched straight in and was standing in the kitchen waiting for me with his arms folded and a grim expression on his face.

'What the hell,' he said, 'is going on?'

I shrugged and went to put the kettle on, more to hide my nervousness than anything else. As it boiled I went through the scenario of the night before, while Chay listened carefully and without comment. I continued with my thoughts on the matter as I made tea in a pot without bothering to ask him if he preferred coffee.

'So you see,' I said, 'as far as I'm aware, in the normal way and as I was the petitioner – the one who was wronged,' I explained cruelly and had the satisfaction of watching him flinch, 'the decree absolute should have been applied for by my solicitor and sent to me – just as the decree nisi was. Obviously, from what I was told by the man walking his dog, something happened to the firm

34

at the crucial time, so I doubt whether it was ever applied for.'

'You could have applied for it yourself,' Chay pointed out in what he obviously thought was a reasonable tone.

'I didn't even notice it hadn't arrived,' I countered, 'and, anyway, so could you, instead of waiting until now.'

He nodded, 'Fair enough. So the information I was given was correct?'

'It would seem so,' I agreed coolly. 'Cup of tea?'

'How can you be so calm about it?' He glared at me, and I hid a wry smile and the fact that my hands were shaking as I poured.

'And the point of getting upset and angry would be?' I asked in my most reasonable tone. 'Sugar?'

'Two,' he said grumpily, pulling out a chair and slumping down into it. 'I don't know what Millicent is going to say.'

'Planned an autumn wedding, had she?' I thought I sounded suitably sympathetic.

'She says I've kept her waiting long enough,' he admitted.

'You didn't want to rush into marriage a second time then?' I held out my ringless left hand. 'Well, neither did I. Once was more than enough.'

'I sometimes wonder what went wrong with us.'

'I don't,' I said sharply. 'It's been over for a long time and there's absolutely no point in dwelling on the past.'

'Mmm,' Chay looked thoughtful. 'I suppose you're right.'

'Yes,' I said firmly. 'More tea?'

We sipped in a fairly companionable silence, and then Chay asked, 'What was the name of your firm of solicitors?'

'Amberwell, Whitburn and Misserbell.'

'You couldn't make it up, could you?' He grinned, then asked, 'Have you looked in the yellow pages?'

'Erm, no.' It was such an obvious thing to do, and I wondered why I hadn't thought of it as I went off to fetch the book, mentally kicking myself.

We both leaned over the pages full of advertisements for legal firms almost, but not quite, touching. I could smell a faint hint of cologne but I didn't recognize it as one Chay had used in days gone by, which was hardly surprising because I didn't use the same perfume as I had back in those long-ago days of our marriage either.

'Nothing even remotely similar, is there?' He sounded despondent again. 'Do you think it's worth us driving over there – you know, where they used to be – just in case?'

'Just in case of *what*?' I demanded, adding sarcastically, 'Just in case they've miraculously reappeared and taken up residence again?'

'You might just have been mistaken.' Chay sounded sulky.

'Oh, you mean I might have mistaken a firm of solicitors for a medical centre? Give me a break, Chay.' I realized too late that I had called him by the pet name that I hadn't used in years and was immediately angry with myself, though he probably hadn't even noticed. 'And in case you're wondering I looked at every building in the bloody road, and got soaked in the process, just in case I had got it wrong.'

'Of course you did. Sorry. Just clutching at straws really.'

We looked at each other in a moment of mutual understanding, which turned to a look of horror when the front door slammed.

'Megan,' we mouthed, just as she came through the kitchen door and stopped dead.

'Dad,' she said, staring at him as if she'd never seen him before. 'I thought that looked like your pick-up outside, but thought it couldn't possibly be. What are you doing here?'

'Erm. . . .' Chay cleared his throat and hesitated, I held my breath and willed him not to tell her the truth, but wasn't quite sure why. 'I was passing and popped in on the off chance to see if I could take you out to lunch.'

I almost applauded. It wasn't totally credible but neither was it beyond the realms of possibility.

'Really?' Megan stared at him, her eyebrows raised as high as they would go. 'Dressed like that? And waiting here – with Mum? Why didn't you just ring?'

There were no flies on our daughter, none at all. I felt I had to wade in to help as I watched Chay floundering.

'He really was just passing – erm – on his way back from seeing a customer – an elderly client who was too concerned to wait until Monday – and I, well, I was out the front – erm – oiling the gate. You know it's been creaking, it kept you awake when it blew open the other night.' Hearing myself gabbling, I shut up abruptly.

'You need to use a little more then,' Megan advised, 'because it was still creaking just as loudly when I came through it just now.'

'I'd better do it again,' I agreed meekly, doubting that we had fooled her for a moment.

'Lunch, then?' Chay queried, valiantly sticking to his lame story. 'Have to be somewhere a bit spit-and-sawdust, though.' He indicated his scruffy clothes ruefully. 'I dressed for an emergency that wasn't.'

'OK, but I can't be out too long. I came back early to start packing my stuff for university.' My stomach lurched at the thought of an imminent departure that I really wasn't looking forward to, and I almost missed Megan's following up that statement with the suggestion, 'Why doesn't Mum come with us – since you're clearly getting along so much better these days?'

Chay and I almost fell over each other in an effort to get across reasons why this wasn't such a good idea. He had come in his pick-up full of work paraphernalia and could only just about squeeze Megan in. I had an urgent order to finish off and my accounts to do.

'We can go in Mum's car, you'll have plenty of time to finish the order when we get back and the accounts can wait one more day. You would have to cook anyway,' she reminded me, 'so eating out will save you time actually.' She saved the guilt trip until last. 'Think how nice it will be for me to share a meal with *both* of my parents. I don't think that's ever happened before in my memory.'

We gave in reasonably gracefully. I even thought it must be worth a couple of hours of discomfort in the company of my ex-husband to see the sheer delight on Megan's face. Almost my ex-husband, I corrected myself and wondered if it was possible to go back, years later, and complete a divorce that no one had bothered to finalize. They probably assumed we had changed our minds, and I supposed that might happen quite a lot.

One thing was certain in my mind: we couldn't let Megan find out we were technically still married because, judging by her smiles at simply seeing the two of us together, it could open up a whole can of worms. I had no intention of bringing back to life those long forgotten childhood wishes that we might be a 'proper' family, living together in domestic harmony.

I slipped on a jacket and found a comb in my handbag. I passed it wordlessly to Chay, who made a good attempt to smooth his hair into some kind of style.

'This is fun,' Megan said gleefully, as we climbed into my elderly Escort. I thought she was gently laughing at us as she got into the back seat and closed the door firmly, leaving Chay little choice but to get in the front with me.

'Where to?' I started the engine and waited while they debated the pros and cons of this pub or that one and then followed their directions to a shabby little back-street pub on the edge of Brankstone, advertising Sunday roasts on the board outside. 'Well,' I said as we stepped

39

inside, 'you do bring us to the best places, don't you, Charlie?'

'I'm sure the food is great.' He nodded confidently. 'That's how these little places keep going. It's certainly busy enough.'

We managed to bag a table tucked away in the corner and Chay went off to order for us all after taking our preferences and refusing my offer to pay.

'This is nice, isn't it?' Megan's brown eyes, so like Chay's, sparkled.

'Mmm.' I didn't want to spoil her pleasure, but felt I just had to remind her. 'Just don't expect this to be a regular occurrence.'

'I won't,' she promised, 'but if it never happens again, it will be a nice memory. What did he want, anyway?'

'Who?' I said, knowing perfectly well, but playing for time and praying for inspiration.

'Dad. Who do you think? He never comes into the house when I'm there, never mind when I'm not.'

'He told you, he wanted to take you for lunch.'

'Mu-um.' Her tone left me in no doubt that she hadn't been fooled at all.

I fished around again for inspiration and came up with something that would have to do. 'He has a surprise up his sleeve; you know, what with you going off to university. He wanted to talk it over with me.'

'Really?' Megan's eyes were wide and she seemed totally convinced this time. 'What is it?'

Well, she had me there, but I rallied. 'If I told you what

it is it wouldn't be a surprise, now, would it?'

'Oooh, a present or a treat, I wonder which? How exciting.'

Thank goodness Chay arrived then with our drinks. Diet coke for Megan, who certainly didn't need to drink diet anything, white wine for me and red for Chay, which surprised me as he'd always used to be a lager man.

'What are you two talking about?'

'About me going to university,' Megan said brightly, 'and how much Mum is going to miss me. You'll have to pop over again, Dad, and give her some company.'

'Megan,' my tone was sharp, 'I'm not exactly friendless, you know. Don't make it sound as if I don't have a social life.'

Actually, we both knew I didn't have much of one because I always said I preferred to work, but wisely Megan stayed quiet, apart from informing us she was just off to powder her nose.

Watching her walk away, Chay observed, 'She's a stunner, isn't she? So much like you at that age. You have the exact same shade of hair, and hers is long with curls, just the way you used to wear yours.'

He'd thought I was a stunner? Well, I guessed he must have since he'd been so desperate to marry me. I'd been head over heels in love with him, too, though it was hard to imagine how it was now that he was little more than a stranger – albeit a rather nice looking one still. I'd have been lying to myself to say otherwise.

'What are we going to do, Charlie? We can't let Megan

41

know we're still married or she will be working out ways to get us back together and planning our silver wedding party before you know it.' He threw back his dark head and laughed, and I found myself hiding a smile as I reminded him with mock severity, 'It's not funny, you know.'

Suddenly serious, he agreed, 'I know, but I haven't a clue where to start, have you? I have no experience of divorce – only ours, and look what a mess we've made of that.'

At least he had stopped blaming it all on me, I was pleased to note, and that made me mellow a bit towards him. 'I'm sure it will be simple enough to sort out.'

'What will?' Megan had come back without either of us noticing.

'None of your business, young lady,' I told her. 'We'll talk about this later,' I said to Chay, realizing we were going to have to be a lot more careful if we didn't want our daughter making efforts to put back together a marriage that had fallen apart more years ago than I cared to remember.

The sooner this particular skeleton stopped rattling and went back into the cupboard, never to be seen again, the better.

CHAPTER FOUR

Apart from warning Chay by email that Megan was expecting some kind of a surprise from him prior to her starting at university, together with a brief explanation as to how that had come about, we had no contact. In fact, for the next two weeks, nothing further was done about looking into finalizing the divorce either, because all of my energies went into helping Megan get ready for university. First things first and, as the marriage had remained intact all this time, I figured that a few more days would make no difference.

From the moment her open suitcase landed on the bed, right after the family lunch that I had endured for her sake, it was all systems go, as I washed and ironed what appeared to be every single item in her wardrobe and raided my airing cupboard for towels and bedding for her student accommodation. We shopped for more must-have garments and those we couldn't find were swiftly made up to her exacting requirements.

'Are you really going to need all of this? Anyone would think you were leaving home for ever,' I said, staring in dismay at the two large suitcases and numerous boxes bursting their contents all over her bedroom with still another week to go. 'You'll be home for half-term next month, won't you?'

'Midwifery isn't just any old university course, you know,' Megan reminded me solemnly. 'We'll be out on community placements before Christmas and we won't be taking long holidays or turning up for lectures just when we feel like it, either. This is going to be three years of hard slog and things like half term won't even come into it.'

I suddenly felt bereft, as if my daughter was going off to war and not just to a university a mere train ride away. I could have burst into tears, and found myself comparing it to Megan's first day at school – only a million times worse, because she wasn't five years old any more and she wouldn't be coming home at the end of each day.

Then I was angry. Why did she have to apply to a university so far from home when there was one with an excellent reputation just up the road from where we were living? I stomped off down the stairs and threw yet another armful of washing into the machine with such force that some of it fell out again. Among the pants and trainer socks I found myself picking up the teddy that had been Megan's favourite from when she was a baby.

I held him to my nose, remembering when he used to smell of Johnson's baby shampoo and talcum powder;

44

now, instead, the distinctive scent of Tresemmé hair products and a favoured Calvin Klein perfume that was essentially Megan, reminded me that she was no longer a baby or even a little girl. My daughter was all grown up these days, preparing to spread her wings and go out into the big wide world.

Realizing that my job was almost over and the rest would be up to Megan was very hard to accept and my tears fell on to the bear's soft brown fur.

'Hey, what's all this?' Megan crouched down beside me. 'Don't tell me you're going to miss me?'

I blinked furiously, threw the bear into the washing machine, added detergent and set the programme while regaining control of my emotions. I managed to do it so well that I was even able to laugh as I said, 'Miss you? You must be joking. What is there to miss? Hot water and the last of the milk all used up in the mornings, never getting to choose which programme to watch on TV or what music to listen to and no more playing gooseberry to you and Tom. Like I said, what is there to miss?'

'You'll miss me reminding you that it's past midnight and you should be in bed instead of still sewing,' Megan pointed out, 'and reminding you to eat when you've worked all day to get a rush order finished. You'll definitely miss my cheese on toast. Oh, don't start crying again, just think how great it will be to have the house to yourself and neat as a new pin all the time without me here to mess it up and drop stuff everywhere.'

'That's true.' I managed a watery smile. 'Now,' I said

briskly, 'what's still on your list of things to do?'

'I don't think I ever had one.' She grinned. 'I'm not as organized as you. When do you think Dad will be round with my surprise? He's running out of time.'

'Surprise?' I looked up from peeling potatoes for yet another shepherd's pie. Megan had insisted she couldn't get enough of her favourite meals before she had to start catering for herself.

'Yeah, you know. You told me about it in the pub the other day when we were having lunch with Dad. He'd come round that day to discuss it with you. I must say,' she added, sounding impressed, 'I'm amazed you've managed to keep it a secret all this time because you're not the best at that, are you? Remember that bike you bought when I was ten and hid so carefully, but didn't notice you'd dropped the pump in the middle of the hall, along with details of cycling proficiency tests?'

I was glad Megan had drifted off the subject of her Dad's surprise, but I knew she wouldn't forget and could only hope that Chay hadn't either. I wondered what on earth he was going to come up with and whether it was up to me to remind him that he had better come up with something.

Everything was cooking nicely, the cheese topping on the shepherd's pie bubbling, Megan's favourite vegetables steaming and Tom had just arrived, when there was a commotion outside and the sound of a car horn tooting excessively. The three of us moved as one to look out of the sitting room window to see what all the noise was about.

'Wow,' said Tom and ran to open the front door to let a grinning Chay stride in.

'Well,' he said, 'what do you think?'

'Oh. My. God,' Megan breathed, 'is that for me?'

'All yours, if you want it,' Chay confirmed, walking back down the path with his arm around his daughter – our daughter.

My first thought was how generous he was being – not that he had ever been anything else with Megan – and my second was that he could at least have discussed buying Megan a car of her own with me first.

At the kerb stood a bright blue Volkswagen Beetle. It wasn't brand new, but it wasn't very old either. A yellow gerbera near the dashboard stood in the holder made for the purpose, and Megan ooh-ed and ah-ed over every little detail, while Tom hung admiringly over the engine beneath the opened bonnet.

Chay stood next to me watching them with a smile on his face and then he looked at me and frowned at my doubtful expression.

'You don't mind, do you?' he asked. 'Only I racked my brain for what this surprise was going to be and this seemed the perfect solution. Megan is going to need a reliable run-around to get her back and forth to her hospital and community placements. I don't fancy her having to depend on public transport when she's on nights or going out late to someone in labour.'

About to ask him why he hadn't thought to discuss the purchase with me first, I suddenly realized it was a ridiculous thing to say, when we hadn't discussed anything much at all for years.

'And neither do I,' I responded quickly, forcing a smile. 'Megan is a good little driver, but she should get a bit more practice in before she drives off into the wide blue yonder. I know she passed her test first go, but she only gets behind of the wheel of my Escort fairly infrequently.'

'All taken care of. I've booked her on a refresher course at the end of the week. It will take up most of her day but will make sure she's safe to be let out on her own.'

I could have kissed him for his foresight, but remembered who he was just in time. Then I gave a sudden shriek and rushed back into the house.

When I turned back from where I was bent over the open oven door, it was to find them, all three of them, standing in the doorway staring at me. I was mortified to think they had all been staring at my backside and just hoped there had been nothing like a builder's bum on show.

'What?' I said, 'What?'

'Well,' Megan spoke first, 'you screamed and ran inside. What were we supposed to think? I thought you were hurt or there had been an explosion.'

I laughed then, and indicated the charred shepherd's pie. 'Just a bit of a disaster, I suddenly realized our dinner was burning. It's ruined.'

Peering round me, Megan insisted, 'I like it like that, a bit crunchy on the top. Run out and lock the car, please Tom, while I help Mum dish up. You'll stay, won't you,

Dad? Feeding you is the least we can do after such a fantastic surprise, isn't it, Mum?'

What could I do but agree, and try to convince myself that this wasn't becoming a habit? Megan would be gone soon, then we could sort out the divorce once and for all, and Chay and I need never see one other again – except perhaps when Megan graduated and when she married.

I refused the offer of joining them for the test run, insisting that I would stay behind to clear up and get some of the ironing done, then I felt lonely and disgruntled as I had to watch them driving away and wished perversely that I had gone. I thought grumpily that they could have tried harder to persuade me to go along, which was ridiculous, not to mention petty. I was never this contrary and really didn't know what was the matter with me lately.

Having Martin phone to apologize and tell me how much he missed me was a soothing balm to my pride and eased my self-inflicted solitude, probably making me warmer and more forgiving than he deserved.

'A quick drink,' he pleaded, when I said I had too much to do to go out. 'I promise I won't keep you out for long. I'll pick you up in ten minutes.'

'Half an hour,' I insisted, 'and I'll meet you there, but it really won't be for long. I still have a lot to do before Meggie leaves for university.'

He gave in fairly graciously, which wasn't much like Martin, who was far too used to getting his own way, I sometimes thought.

I practically threw the dishes in the dishwasher and set it going, before racing upstairs to drag a comb through my hair, touch up my lipstick and bemoan the fact there really was no time to shower and change. Still, if my standard garb of jeans and T-shirt weren't to Martin's taste he would either have to like it or lump it, since meeting up with precious little warning was his idea.

'Darling.' Martin swept me into his arms and kissed me with greater enthusiasm than I had come to expect from him in recent weeks. Perhaps ignoring his hissy fit over my meeting with Chay and not bothering to contact him since might actually have been a good move. In truth, that hadn't been intentional; I had just been too busy to think very much about it or to let his silence bother me unduly. Perhaps when he said jump I really should stop asking how high in future.

I sipped the chilled Pinot he handed me and asked him how he had been. We chatted amicably for a while about his job in the city and he showed unusual interest in the orders for my latest creations. The change made me realize, probably for the first time in our relationship, that Martin's conversation usually centred almost entirely on Martin.

'So,' he said after a while and in a deceptively casual tone, 'how did the meeting with the ex go?'

'It was fine,' I said carelessly, and left it at that.

'Just fine, is that it? Will you be seeing him again, or aren't I supposed to ask?'

I noticed Martin was starting to sound tetchy and it

made me annoyed. After all, I didn't question him about his ex and what happened between them. To be honest, he wouldn't have allowed such an intrusion into something he would see as absolutely none of my business and I decided suddenly that neither would I.

Up until now he'd had no reason to be concerned about an ex-husband who didn't figure very much at all in my life; perhaps this would even things up a bit. It wasn't necessary for him to know that Chay was back in my life for one reason and one reason only – and that was to be rid of me for good.

'He is Megan's father and whether I see Charlie again or not doesn't really concern you, does it, Martin? We're both free agents, as you've told me often enough. He's my ex; that doesn't mean we can't be friends, does it?'

I realized belatedly that I had almost quoted one of Martin's own, oft-repeated, platitudes back at him, and by the look on Martin's face, he realized it, too. He opened his mouth and then closed it again. He didn't look very pleased, but struggled to put a brave face on it.

'You're right, of course.' He smiled and changed the subject. 'So when can I take you out for a meal? Shall I book a table at Isabelle's for Saturday?'

'That's when Megan moves into her hospital accommodation, ready for the start of her course. I was hoping to go up there and see her settled in, so it will have to be a no, I'm afraid. Perhaps the week after?'

I had never refused a date with Martin in all the months I had been seeing him, not ever. I had always gone out of my way to accommodate any of the precious time he chose to bestow on me, including cancelling appointments and stopping mid-job when necessary. He looked as shocked as I felt. I wondered suddenly what I was playing at and he must have been doing the same. Only very recently I had thought myself extremely lucky that he appeared to want me in his life, when it was quite obvious he could have his pick of any women he wanted.

There was no doubt that Martin was what would – in any sensible woman's eyes – be termed a real catch. Divorced for some time, he was exceptionally good-looking, well-heeled from his dealings in the city and living in penthouse overlooking the sea with a Porsche parked in the underground garage. He was charming, no doubt about that – when he wanted to be – and for the moment he obviously did want to be.

'Well, of course you'll want to see Megan settled,' he agreed, 'but Saturday week seems a hell of a long time to wait to see you again.'

I was so surprised that I almost reminded him that we often went for a month and, at times even two, between dates. Instead, I simply said mildly, 'I'll have a lot of catching up to do, I seem to have spent for ever making sure she has everything she needs, but then it's not every day your only daughter leaves home.'

'She is eighteen,' he reminded me, quite kindly.

'Yes,' I said, '*only* eighteen and I want to make sure she's all right.'

'Of course,' he agreed mildly and I might have

imagined the flicker of annoyance in his pale blue eyes as he agreed, 'Saturday week it is, then. I'll look forward to that. You're not going already, are you?' he added quickly when I stood up and reached for my bag.

'I said an hour and it's been longer. I really do have a lot to do. No doubt I'll have a lot of time on my hands once Megan is at university, but right now I have far too much to do and precious little time to do it in.'

I felt the familiar lurch in the pit of my stomach that the thought of Megan going always gave me and I didn't really welcome Martin's advances when he saw me to my car. His kisses were deep, his breathing heavy, and there was no doubt that he was becoming aroused, but instead of revelling in the fact that he obviously desired me, for once all I could think about was getting home.

'Where have you been until this time?' My daughter sounded so uncannily like me that I had to hide a smile.

'It's,' I checked my watch and pointed out mildly, 'a few minutes after nine thirty.'

'But you *said* you had a lot to do and that's why you couldn't come out in my new car.'

'Yes, I did, and that's why I need to get a move on now.' I pulled the ironing board out of the cupboard and set it up with the usual clatter, then retrieved the iron from its shelf and plugged it in, before collecting the basket of freshly laundered clothes from the hall cupboard.

'Where have you been, then?' Megan had her arms folded in a most un-Megan-like way. 'Dad waited ages for you to come back.' Her tone was almost accusing.

'Why?' I said, without looking up from the blouse I was pressing.

'What do you mean, why? I don't know. He probably wanted a word or something. He is your—'

'*Ex*-husband,' I put in helpfully.

I thought I had made my point. I hoped so, because it wasn't like Megan to question me about how I spent my time and she had never tried to put a guilt trip on me. I just hoped she wasn't getting any ideas about Chay and me reconciling after all these years just because he had been round to the house a couple of times. I could only feel great relief that she knew nothing about the fact that we might just still be married.

CHAPTER FIVE

I could barely hide my satisfaction when it became apparent that all the things Megan wanted to take with her were not going to fit into the Volkswagen.

'You'll need to keep your back window clear,' I told her firmly, when the boxes on the back seat reached the roof inside the car and would obviously be obscuring her vision.

'But I need it all,' she wailed, standing on the pavement with her hands on her enviably slim hips.

'I can take some of it in mine,' I offered, happy to be given an excuse to go and see where she was going to be living, even though we'd already had a tour of the accommodation block months ago.

'Or mine.' We both turned to find Chay standing behind us and he added – I assumed by way of explanation for his presence, 'Just checking that you didn't need any extra help.'

'I can manage,' I said sharply, determined not to be

done out of the trip I so badly wanted to make. 'I don't mind making the drive.'

'Neither do I.' He looked at my Escort, which admittedly had seen better days, and suggested quietly, 'We could both go – in my car. Luckily I brought the four by four.' He indicated the silver vehicle standing by the kerb behind my car. 'I think we're going to need it – though by the look of all those boxes, the pick-up might have been an even better choice.'

I was about to insist on driving myself, that I was sure the boxes would fit, to tell him there was no need for both of us to go. Then I realized, perhaps from the hopeful way he was looking at me, that he was as desperate to see Megan safely settled as I was. My mouth snapped shut, and I gave an abrupt nod.

'Actually, that would be great, then Tom could make the trip with me and get a lift back with you two. His course doesn't start until next week,' Megan added, 'and it might be ages before we see each other after that.'

How could we refuse? It was only natural they would want to spend as much time as they could in each other's company before they went their separate ways for the foreseeable future.

'I'll give him a ring,' she said happily, retrieving her mobile phone from her pocket, flipping it open and almost skipping up the path as she waited for Tom to answer.

'Thank you,' Chay said.

I didn't ask for what because it was obvious we both knew. I shrugged, 'That's OK. I don't mind paying for my share of the petrol – or I could buy lunch,' I added when he looked affronted.

'Best start getting some of this into my boot and on to the back seat then.' He hefted a box, grimacing at the weight, and I followed him with a lighter one. 'She will be all right,' he said.

'I know.' I handed him my box and watched him pack it into his car.

'But you're going to miss her.'

I nodded, keeping my eyes wide in case they had the temerity to fill with silly tears. 'A lot.'

'Me, too,' he said, 'though I do understand it will be worse for you, with her living under the same roof and all.'

I hadn't expected his understanding and I couldn't help but be touched by it. However, I didn't need any encouragement to become maudlin about the imminent parting, so I became brisk.

'We'd better get this lot loaded up, or we won't be there until midnight,' I stated, bundling a rolled-up duvet into his arms and then rushing to rescue the little bear from where it had fallen from an over-filled box and into the road.

'I can't believe she still has that.'

Chay took the toy from me and sat it tenderly in the corner of the parcel shelf in his car so that it faced out on the world. I wondered if he was remembering, as I was, the day we had bought it together for our beautiful little daughter. It was one of the few happy memories I had amid the sad ones as our marriage fell apart.

There were some long uncomfortable silences as we set off on the long journey to where our daughter would start a long journey of her own towards the career she had set her mind on. I found myself already thinking longingly of the journey back when we would at least have Tom in the car with us.

At one point Chay cleared his throat awkwardly and looked at me sideways, as if he was brewing up to say something he didn't think I was going to like. Stabbing a guess at what that might be, I got in first.

'If you're going to ask me how the search for the disappearing solicitor is going,' I said flatly, 'I can tell you that it isn't going anywhere at the moment, because I've had quite enough to do with getting Megan properly organized. It's too far for her to run home if she finds she's forgotten anything.'

As soon as I'd said it I was cross that I'd reminded myself of the distance there would be between us, and so upset that I just wanted to burst into tears.

'I wasn't,' Chay said, adding, 'Going to ask, I mean.'

'It will get sorted,' I told him, and I meant it. We were over, done, finished long ago. The fact that we still needed the legal stamp that would finally end the marriage was hardly here or there, really – no more than a formality.

I reached out and turned the radio on, hoping to fill the awkward silences with music and chat that would distract us from the yawning chasm between us. Unfortunately, there was a golden hour playing from a year when things had still been good between us and the tension was palpable as we fought against remembering all kinds of things we would be better off forgetting.

'Is Millicent OK about all this time you've been spending doing stuff for Meggie – you know, and buying her the car and everything?'

I introduced the subject of his girlfriend purposely in order to break the spell the music was starting to weave around us. I was pleased to note that it worked immediately.

'She's fine,' Chay snapped, reaching out to flick the radio to another station where the music sounded more to Megan's taste than either of ours. 'Why wouldn't she be? She has always known and accepted that my daughter has to come first.'

Ooh, a bit of a touchy subject, I felt, and wondered whether Millicent really was as cool as Chay seemed to believe about being relegated to second place. I would guess, perhaps unfairly, that she was probably highly delighted that Megan was moving so far away and would think a car was a small price to pay if she could at last have Chay to herself. Of course, I could have been wrong and probably shouldn't have formed an opinion based on the very few comments my daughter had made about the woman from time to time.

Careful not to let any of these thoughts show in the expression that I kept deliberately bland, I said lightly, 'She's obviously a very understanding lady.'

His own expression was unreadable as he grunted

something that could have been anything, making me wonder even more if all really was well in their relationship.

None of my business, I reminded myself smartly, assuring myself that the very next thing on my agenda would be getting the divorce paperwork sorted out so that their marriage could go ahead and make Chay safely out of bounds.

Now, what the hell did that mean? I tried to ignore the heat that suffused my face and hoped I wasn't blushing. Out of bounds – Chay had been out of bounds to me for many years and I hadn't given a thought in all that time that it could ever be otherwise – until now. I quickly reminded myself that I was just looking at things the way that Megan would if she found out we were still married, and that made me feel marginally better.

'Does she mind?'

I realized belatedly that Chay had been speaking to me, probably for some time. 'Sorry, what was that?' I belatedly turned to look at him, happy that the blush on my face had subsided, and added, 'I was miles away, going through Meggie's university lists in my head – though I know it's a bit late to be turning back now if we've forgotten anything. Most things can be posted, though I'm relieved that I know for sure the duvet made it into the car. Think of the waste of brown wrapping paper – never mind the cost.'

Chay laughed, having regained his usual good humour, and he pointed out, 'That's what I was asking you about, the pet name Meggie. Does she not mind you still using it? It makes her sound about three years old again.'

I found myself laughing, too. 'I only ever say it when we're alone. She'd be mortified if I used such a babyish name in company, but I think secretly she quite likes it sometimes – especially when she's tired or poorly.'

'Oh-oh, Megan is flashing her headlights at me.' Glancing in the rear-view mirror, Chay suddenly touched the brakes and slowed down. 'I hope nothing is wrong with the car. I made sure it was checked and serviced.'

'Look,' I pointed, 'we're coming up to the services. Do you think they want us to turn in and get a break? We must be about halfway.'

'You're right, they're indicating.' He promptly did the same, took the slip road and eased smoothly into a parking spot that had just been vacated practically at the entrance. Chay had always been lucky like that and I'd used to joke that he had his own parking angel. I bit my lip before I could do the same on this occasion.

By the time Megan and I had visited the washrooms and the shop, the guys had grabbed a table and had pots of tea and sandwiches waiting for us – egg and cress for Megan and cheese and pickle for me.

'Oh, Mum prefers. . . .' Megan began, but I stopped her quickly, saying, 'It's fine,' and tucking in rather than make the point that my taste in sandwiches had changed rather a lot over the years.

Still mentally ticking things off in my brain, I asked, 'You did get time to see Grandma, didn't you?'

'Popped in, phoned,' Megan checked off on her fingers, adding, 'I only just persuaded her that joining us on this trip would be a bad idea. She's talking of getting Skype and joining Facebook so that she can talk to me and keep up with my news.'

'A silver-surfer in the making.' Chay smirked. 'Obviously a bit more computer savvy than her daughter, then. Megan says you detest them.'

'PCs are a necessary evil as far as I'm concerned, not for fun, and the less I have to do with them the better I like it. Mum has more time on her hands,' I pointed out, refusing to rise to the bait, 'and obviously an interest in having a hundred friends she never knew she had, who clearly can't be bothered to keep in touch in any other way. I have better things to do with my time – like talking to people face to face.'

'Not a fan then, Tessa?' Tom asked.

I shook my head and shrugged. 'It shows, huh? That probably makes me old-fashioned, but I really can't be bothered. I can see that the Internet has its uses and the website you set up for me has paid dividends, even though I never bother to update it, because people at least know what I do and how to contact me.'

'You have a website?' Chay looked impressed.

I resisted the urge to make a sarcastic reply, such as not still living in the Dark Ages even if I didn't fancy twittering away my time, and nodded. 'Tessa's Togs – not very original, I know, but I do well enough.'

'She'll do even better with me out of her hair,' Megan

said. She drank the rest of her tea and got to her feet. 'So let's go and get me settled ready for the start of my course on Monday and give Mum her freedom.'

It was a freedom I wasn't looking forward to. I had relished being a mum from the day Megan was born – seeing her as the one thing Chay and I had got absolutely right – and would have preferred a few more years of having her living under my watchful eye. However, I managed to put on a huge act by singing a couple of lines from *Freedom*, the popular Wham song from the eighties, as we left the restaurant.

I was grimly determined to keep things light-hearted right up to the moment I headed for home, leaving my daughter to get on with her new and exciting life. After that I could weep, wail and worry to my heart's content, but she would never know and be put under pressure to be constantly in touch to check that I was all right.

All too soon we really were ready to head for home. I had to admit that after checking the accommodation that Megan would be sharing with three other new students I did feel marginally better about leaving her. When we briefly met Kate, who was a similar age to Megan, Sarah who was a year older and Jill who was in her early twenties, I felt comforted by how well-matched they seemed and I did think they should do well together and become good friends.

The accommodation itself was in an old building, but it had obviously been given a recent makeover and was smart and clean. Each girl had her own reasonably sized room with bed, wardrobe, chest of drawers and desk, Internet connection was available, the bathrooms were en suite and there was a shared living room and kitchen. The building had CCTV and security fobs to enter the building and the flats, which was a comfort, and there was a coin-operated launderette on the ground floor. There was parking available with a permit, which had already been arranged for Megan.

I helped stow all Megan's things away neatly, and tried not to think about the mess the room would soon be in without me there to constantly pick up behind her. Smiling steadfastly through the pain of the imminent departure and separation until my face actually hurt, I even managed a joke about being pleased to receive dirty laundry by parcel post, keeping up the cheery exterior through the hugs and reminders to enjoy every moment until the car had at least pulled away from the kerb. In the end I could only be thankful that Tom had decided not to return with us, but would go on to stay with nearby relatives for a few days, when my determinedly cheery exterior disintegrated at a speed that was frightening and exceedingly embarrassing.

I was still waving energetically when the tears began to flow, and sobbing hysterically by the time we had left the city and headed for the motorway. The thought of the very empty nest that awaited me at the end of the journey was almost more than I could bear.

CHAPTER SIX

To Chay's absolute credit, he said not a word of either comfort or sarcasm, but just concentrated on his driving while I howled the miles away huddled in the passenger seat.

I knew I was being ridiculous and was well aware that hundreds, possibly thousands of other mothers all over the UK were currently facing what I was facing, as their children left home to go to university or college. The majority were probably making a better job of accepting the situation and with far better grace than I presently was.

I was carrying on as if my daughter had died – and what a chilling thought that was, and a deeply sobering one. I should stop this, and stop it right now, be grateful that my separation from my daughter was at least not a permanent one. For goodness' sake, I could pick up the phone and speak to her every single day if I wanted to, so what the hell was wrong with me?

I sniffed, hiccuped and, as I surfaced from my miserable huddle, with my face probably smeared with make-up and snot, I realized that Chay was bringing the car to a halt and that we were on the end of a traffic jam that looked as if it went on for miles.

Shocked out of my self-inflicted misery, I asked, 'My God, what happened?'

'Must be an accident ahead.' He fiddled with the radio, probably looking for a traffic report, and then looked at me. 'Are you OK?' He didn't even look disgusted, for which I was grateful.

'I will be,' I tried to make it sound as if I was certain, and resisted the urge to let the tears that still threatened spill over again. 'I'm sorry to make such a show of myself. It won't happen again. You do think she'll be all right, don't you – our Meggie?'

'She'll be fine.' Chay's tone was reassuringly firm. 'The world is her oyster. She's confident and focused on what she wants. You've done a great job bringing her up.'

I wasn't just being generous by insisting, 'You must take half of the credit for that.'

'Not really.' Chay looked kind of sad for a moment, as he continued, 'You had the sleepless nights and all the childhood ailments to deal with. I just got the fun days out.'

'A bit more than that, I think. You've been a great dad.'

'Thank you.'

'You're welcome.'

We lapsed into silence and stared out at the lines of

traffic ahead of us and didn't need to turn around to know there were now long queues behind us as well. Chay turned off the engine.

This was the last thing either of us needed, I acknowledged, aware of a slight feeling of panic. Being forced to sit in a confined space for God knew how long and make polite chitchat, after years of barely being able to pass the time of day in a civilized manner, wasn't funny at all. At least I supposed the missing decree had forced us to make the sort of effort recently that we probably should have been making years ago for Megan's sake.

In the end I said something of the sort out loud and wondered, 'Should we have tried harder?'

'How do you mean? Tried harder to work things out between us for Meggie?'

I shook my head, 'It was probably too late for that even before she was born. Did we really think having a child would bring us together? It was like putting a sticking plaster on a broken limb by then. But we could have tried harder to get along for her sake, once she was born, even after we split up.'

'God, she was beautiful, wasn't she?'

'When she was born?' I smiled at a memory that we both shared through the proud eyes of being her parents. 'She was absolutely gorgeous.'

'Red-haired and dark-eyed just like her mum.' Chay was smiling, too.

'Auburn,' I corrected, 'her hair is auburn and so is mine.'

'Auburn,' he allowed.

I fished in my bag for some wipes, wondering why I hadn't thought to clean up my face before this instead of sitting there looking a complete fright. Acknowledging that it was nothing Chay hadn't seen before didn't help because it was different when you were a couple. These days we were comparative strangers and, anyway, youthful tears were so much more attractive than middle-aged ones.

'What happened to us, Tess?'

I pretended to consider Chay's question, while pulling a brush through the tangles of my hair. 'We married too young and against everyone's advice,' I reminded him eventually, 'and then were too bloody-minded to admit defeat or even ask for help when the going got tough. I think that pretty much sums it up, don't you?'

'Getting married at eighteen without a penny to our name probably wasn't one of our best ideas,' he conceded, without too much hesitation.

'It was madness,' I said firmly. 'It wasn't even as if we had to or anything.'

'It just seemed like a good idea at the time,' Chay suggested with a level of flippancy that didn't impress me at all.

'Well, it wasn't?' I said harshly. 'Whose idea was it, anyway?'

'I think it was your dad's.'

I put a hand up to my mouth no doubt smudging the lipstick I had just that minute applied. 'Oh, yes.'

I could picture my dad, red in the face and fuming, as we stood hand in hand in front of him and insisted we wanted to get engaged. 'You're nowt but kids,' he had yelled, temper accentuating his strong northern accent. 'You've seen nothing of the world yet, but you think you know it all.' Then he had thrown his hands up in the air and demanded furiously, 'Why don't you just get married and have done with it?'

He hadn't meant it, of course, and was just trying, in his rather heavy-handed way to make us see sense. No one could have been more shocked than he was when we went off and did just that.

'He overreacted, of course, but can you imagine how we would feel if Meggie and Tom did that to us?' The very thought horrified me.

'With our track record I do think we would have to be a bit more understanding and not just go off at the deep end,' Chay pointed out, and I had to agree.

His mobile phone rang then and he got out among the stationary traffic to take the call, so I guessed it must be from the lovely Millicent. I noticed that a lot of other motorists were also pacing among the cars while they accepted or made calls. I wondered idly whether, technically, they could be charged with using a mobile phone while driving and then went back to contemplating the circumstances that had led to our hasty teenage marriage.

We had thought we were so grown-up and able to make our own decisions, but we had scuppered our own dreams for the future with our hot-headed insistence that we knew best. I'd always been keen on fashion, was already making and designing my own clothes in secondary school and had been accepted on a course at the local college. Chay was lined up for an engineering degree. Instead we were married at the local registrar's office wearing borrowed finery and, having no money for a honeymoon, we went straight out to work – Chay as a labourer on a building site and me at the local factory making swimwear.

The grief we caused our parents didn't bear thinking about even now years later. Refusing their generous offers to live with either of them, we went off and found a run-down flat that was all we could afford to rent. It was three floors up from a busy street, but we were determined to prove wrong everybody who doubted the wisdom of our youthful marriage.

At first it had even been fun as we decorated the shabby rooms of our first home with paint from tins that Chay found discarded at work. Luckily for us, in the eighties, as now, most new houses were painted in neutral colours that lightened the place up considerably. Our furniture was second-hand, our linen and towels came from the local market, as did most of our food.

What did we care? We were lusty and in love and had suddenly gone from snatched sessions of heavy petting on our parents' settees to a double bed and a marriage licence that entitled us to have sex twenty-fours hours a day. Something we took full advantage of.

I blushed, sitting there in the traffic remembering, after a day at work, rushing home where we would tear each other's clothes off the minute we were inside the door. It had been good – so good – between us, so when did it all go wrong – and why?

I hadn't realized that I had spoken out loud until Chay, climbing into the car beside me, suggested, 'Was it when we decided to go all conventional?'

'Always trying to prove everyone wrong, weren't we?'

He nodded. 'Renting a nicer flat would have been a saner idea than going the whole hog and buying a house that we quite obviously couldn't afford. How we scraped up the deposit I'll never know, but the payments really put us under so much pressure, far more than we could ever hope to cope with.'

I remembered it well, feeling so proud that at twenty-one years old we actually owned our own home except that, in reality, all we owned was a few bricks and a hefty and pretty dodgy mortgage. The day we moved in Chay carried me laughing across the threshold, but we soon found that all the joy had disappeared from our marriage, as we struggled to keep on top of the bills.

Long hours of overtime to make ends meet meant we spent little time together, even cuddles became a thing of the past and sex was the last thing on our minds. As we strived to better ourselves it felt as if the soul went out of our relationship. Young as we were, we both knew that if we didn't do something, and soon, the rows and recriminations would soon chip away at the love we

71

shared until there was nothing left. Drastic action was needed and we thought we had found the answer.

Having a child under those circumstances was the most ridiculous idea, but I suppose we were desperate, and for a while it seemed to work. However, the added financial pressure eventually saw the house repossessed and, finally conceding defeat, I moved back in with my parents. Looking back we had done well to last as long as we had.

I still hadn't thought it was over; I just assumed Chay would find us another home, and we would soon be back together. Instead he seemed to just give up on us – or that was the way it had always seemed to me. I had never forgiven him, I realized, and sitting there as the traffic began to flow again I thought that I probably never would.

CHAPTER SEVEN

It must have been only a coincidence, but with the change in my feelings, the temperature in the car dropped noticeably. Chay must have also felt it because he reached out and turned the heater on.

I could actually feel the recent warming in my attitude towards him evaporate as I allowed the bitterness from the past to creep in, and I wondered how I was going to be civil towards him for the rest of the journey. I knew I probably shouldn't put all the blame on him, but I did, convinced he should have tried a lot harder to keep us together. Biting back the bitter accusations wasn't easy, but I did it, the sensible part of me realizing that it was far too late for such recriminations.

However, it seemed prudent to remind him that he had a girlfriend, which I did by asking, 'Millicent was it? On the phone just now? I hope our being caught up in traffic isn't going to mess up any plans you might have for this evening.'

Chay gave me a puzzled look, then said, 'Millicent understands that a delay like this can't be helped. I thought we were talking about us.'

I smiled sweetly and hoped he couldn't see that my teeth were actually gritted. 'That's it though, isn't it, Charlie, there is no "us". There's been no "us" for a very long time.'

My mobile rang then as if right on cue. 'Martin,' I said warmly, very aware of Chay's scowling look. 'How are you?'

'Missing you,' he said, his voice full of innuendo, 'and just wondering how the trip went. It's a hell of a way to have to drive. Has Megan settled in all right?' he managed courteously and then got to the point. 'Are you anywhere near home yet?'

'Nowhere near,' I said regretfully, watching yet another motorway sign crawl by and realizing that at this rate we had zero chance of getting home before the early hours. 'We – um – I got caught up in a tailback from an accident or something. I'm moving now, but only just.' I hoped he hadn't noticed the slip and frowned at Chay, almost daring him to open his mouth and leave me to launch into explanations about why we were travelling together. At that moment I couldn't for the life of me work out why we had thought it was such a good idea.

'That's a shame.' Martin actually sounded dis-appointed, which wasn't like him at all. Never one for letting his feelings show, I had never imagined seeing myself as anywhere near the top of the list of his priorities. 'Look, I'm working away most of the week and I was going to suggest rather than a meal next weekend, we go the whole hog and actually make a weekend of it. Anywhere you like, Devon, the lakes. You choose.'

'A weekend away?' I chanced a sly smile in Chay's direction and the look of disapproval on his face made me even more effusive. 'Oh, Martin that would be lovely, but you choose, you have such good taste.'

'That's a date then.' Martin sounded pleased with my response and went on to promise me a weekend I wouldn't forget. . . . 'For several reasons,' he added huskily.

I returned the phone to my bag and settled back into the passenger seat, feeling smug – and trying not to think too deeply about spending two days with a man I hadn't spent much more than two hours in one go with in all the time I'd known him.

'Martin?' Chay quirked an eyebrow in my direction. 'Been seeing him long?'

'A few months,' I answered casually in a what's-it-got-to-do-with-you kind of tone, wishing I didn't feel pleased at his show of interest when it shouldn't matter to me at all. 'I'm surprised Meggie hasn't mentioned him.'

Ignoring that, Chay queried, 'Serious?'

'Could be.' I refused to be drawn any further and changed the subject to one that should be close to Chay's heart. 'Anyway, we must sort out this decree thing and then you and Millicent can get on and set a date for your wedding.'

'Why do you do that?' Chay demanded, slamming his foot on the brake so that the car behind hooted, even though we were scarcely moving.

'What?' I asked, the picture of innocence.

'Change the subject back to me anytime we're talking about you?'

'Because it was you chasing me to sort out the divorce,' I suggested in what I thought was a perfectly reasonable tone, 'and that's what I will be doing, I can assure you, now that Meggie is safely settled. So you and Millicent could probably safely plan a Christmas wedding.'

'Will you shut up about the bloody divorce and the bloody wedding?' Chay fumed, driving dangerously close to the Mini in front, so that I pressed my foot to the floor, instinctively looking for the brake.

'Don't you speak to me like that.' I suddenly realized I was practically shrieking and had to work to tone it down a bit, 'it's *you* who wants both, remember? I just want to get on with my life.'

'With this bloody Martin, one assumes,' he growled nastily, stopping about a centimetre from the Mini's bumper

'None of your business,' I said through gritted teeth, 'and will you please stop swearing.'

'Or what?'

'Or I'll get out of the car and walk,' I threatened recklessly. 'I don't have to listen to you. We're no longer husband and wife.' As soon as I said the words I realized what I'd said and could have bitten my tongue off.

'Isn't that the whole bloody problem?' he snarled viciously, 'that we *are* still husband and wife?'

'Not for much bloody longer, if I can bloody help it,' I spat, and before he realized my intention, I'd opened the door, stepped out of the car and, slamming the door behind me with all of my might, I started walking purposefully along the hard shoulder.

I could hear Chay shouting something about getting back into the car *right now*. I didn't turn round, not even when the traffic suddenly speeded up a bit and Chay's four by four was right alongside of me, keeping level, and the queue crawling behind were sounding a cacophony of horns.

'Get into the bloody car, love, and sort the argument out at home,' a gruff voice from the almost identical four by four following Chay's advised quite kindly, 'before you get picked up by the police.'

His words brought me to my senses and I suddenly realized what an absolute fool I was making of myself. I didn't need telling that I should have known a lot better at my age. Sheepishly, I got back into the car to cheers and jeers and another orchestra of car horns and could feel my face burning as I slid down low in the seat.

'Sorry,' I muttered eventually. 'That was a really stupid thing to do.'

'I'm sorry, too,' Chay said, surprising me.

'What's happened to us?' I wondered. 'We've barely managed a civil word since the div . . . separation.'

'We've probably been a nightmare for Megan to deal

with,' he agreed ruefully. 'No wonder she was so thrilled when we managed to get through a whole meal without tearing lumps out of each other. I expect she was hoping she'd no longer have the role of go-between.'

'We should try harder, shouldn't we? It's not as if we have to live in each other's pockets. We hardly have to see each other, but imagine how bad it would be for Megan if we couldn't get along for her graduation.' I was beginning to feel increasingly guilty, thinking of what Megan had had to put up with over the years from the pair of us.

'Or her wedding.'

'How awful for our grandchildren.' I grimaced, and then laughed. 'I never saw myself as a grandparent, did you?'

Chay grinned. 'Not exactly, but I do kind of like the idea. Don't you?'

'Yes,' I said, 'I do.'

There was a perceptible thaw in the air between us and even the inevitable gaps in the conversation from that moment on were no longer tense or, for my part, at least, filled with the bitter accusations that could fill a mind, yet remain – for the most part – unsaid.

The traffic slowed and speeded up intermittently, but a journey that was already long enough seemed to become never-ending. Night fell and I offered to take over the driving and then was miffed when Chay refused. It took me all my time not to demand if it was because he didn't trust me behind the wheel of his precious car, though that probably wasn't the case at all.

It was late – or early, depending on which way you looked at it – when we eventually pulled up outside my house. I found myself offering Chay coffee and wasn't sure whether it was out of concern because he was clearly exhausted and still had a – mercifully short – drive ahead of him, or whether I was putting off the inevitable loneliness of a house without Megan in it.

Ridiculous, really, because she wasn't always at home even to sleep, but I had to acknowledge that this time it was different.

Chay hesitated, and I waited for the refusal, and steeled myself to face the empty house like the adult I was. Perhaps he saw my expression, even in the darkened car, or positively even understood my reluctance to walk through the door alone this first time.

'Better make it black,' he said, reaching for the door handle.

I was more grateful than I could say for his solid presence behind me as I walked up the path, slid the key in the front door and stepped into the darkness of the hall. We both blinked when the light came on.

'That was one heck of a journey.' I filled the kettle and offered, 'You can have instant, or perhaps real coffee will be better for keeping you awake?'

'Perhaps it would,' his tone was rueful, 'but I'd be sound asleep before it was ready. Instant will do just fine.'

I put biscuits on a plate and set them in front of him, and then went upstairs, picking up stuff that had been discarded or merely dropped by Megan as she left. I shouldn't have opened her bedroom door and knew it even as I turned the handle. I quickly closed the door again, but it was too late. The room looked abandoned, the bed stripped, and grief hit me so hard that I gasped as if I'd been punched in the stomach, before the tears came.

I didn't hear Chay coming, just felt the welcome warmth as he gathered me into his arms. I made no attempt to pull myself together and to his credit he didn't urge me to do any such thing, but just shushed me like a baby and assured me that everything was going to be fine.

At what point the comfort turned to passion I couldn't have said, or who instigated the kiss that started it all, but what followed was entirely mutual. Gentle kisses became deep and searching, and then wild and hungry. Hands seeking the warmth of bare flesh became impatient and clothes were torn and discarded as we came together, barely making it to my bedroom in the urgency of need, intent only on taking and giving pleasure.

It was over quickly and I came to my senses at a speed that made my head spin, but too late, far too late. I was mortified and Chay couldn't even meet my eyes and we scrambled round for the scattered items of clothing, dressed and went downstairs in complete silence.

As the kettle reboiled I found my tongue and chattered inconsequently, mostly about Megan and her course and when she might be expected home. All the time I was very aware of Chay's total lack of response as he sat at the table behind me and embarrassed by the slight soreness and mild bruising that were the result of our urgent and out-of-control love-making. I couldn't even get on my high horse and accuse him of taking advantage, because he'd have had every right to laugh in my face and I knew it.

I set the cups on the table and sat down, reaching for a biscuit and crunching away with every appearance of enjoyment, determined to give the impression that I wasn't bothered. I was fooling nobody but felt I should at least try, because I wasn't at all sure where we went from here.

'Don't you think we should at least talk about what just happened?' Chay said at last.

Thankfully, by that time I had finally gathered my scattered wits into some semblance of order and I had my response ready.

'Why?' I said, and gave a careful and very careless shrug. 'What did just happen, Chay? A moment of utter madness that meant absolutely nothing to either of us. We were both exhausted after the long and difficult drive, I was upset and not thinking straight. So, no, I don't think we should talk about it, just put it behind us and forget all about it.'

'Just like that?' He was staring at me.

'Just like that,' I said firmly. 'As far as I'm concerned, it never happened.'

'If that's what you want.'

'It is.'

He left soon after and I tidied up and went up to bed, feeling more tired than I could recall ever feeling in my life before.

"It never happened." Brave words that lacked the ring of truth and, coming face to face with my bed with its tangled mess of covers telling its own story, I knew that stripping the bedding was a futile effort and that the vision of us entwined there was going to be forever stamped on my memory.

Even as I set the dial on the washing machine I was wondering how we had even made it to the bed. As I made the bed up with fresh linen, and then showered the scent of him from my skin, I was remembering how being in Chay's arms again had made me feel, and I couldn't dismiss it, or even regret it, no matter how hard I tried.

CHAPTER EIGHT

I slept only fitfully through what remained of the night and then, typically, fell into a deep sleep around dawn and was eventually woken by the doorbell.

'Mum.' I threw open the door wider when I saw who was on the step.

She stared at me in amazement. 'Were you asleep?' she asked.

'Mmm,' I muttered. 'Why? What time is it?'

'Almost eleven o'clock, and I thought you never slept past eight, even at weekends. Here's me thinking you'd be missing Megan and needing some company. Obviously I needn't have bothered.'

'Nonsense, come on in, some company is just what I need today. I didn't get home until the early hours. Hell of a journey back yesterday; some sort of accident or accidents on the motorway caused major hold-ups.'

'Oh, poor you.' Mum bustled into the kitchen saying, as she took off her coat, 'Now have you eaten? Oh, silly me, of course you haven't, you've only just got up. You go and have a shower and leave me to it.' She reached for my one and only apron hanging on the back of the kitchen door, and tied it round her still trim waist.

I went, welcoming the distraction of having my mother around for more reasons than one. By the time I was ready to face the day, there was tea and toast waiting for me, and the washing was pegged on the line.

'Sit down and eat up,' she urged. 'You still look tired, you poor thing. I was amazed to find washing in the machine. When did you do that? You don't usually change your bed at the weekend. You always said weekends weren't for washing unless it was an emergency.'

The sudden surge of extreme heat to my face felt as if it had burst into flames. I hoped my usually observant mother hadn't noticed what must be a very obvious blush as I jumped up and busied myself pouring out more tea.

'I could have done that,' she pointed out.

'I was a bit wired when I got home,' I offered, once I'd had time to think, 'and needed to doing something to make myself wind down.'

'I usually read in bed for a bit,' she offered mildly, 'I find that does the trick.'

'I didn't think of that and, anyway, I didn't have a book handy. Haven't had too much time for reading lately.'

My mother laughed, 'I expect Megan has kept you busy. You're going to miss her, no doubt about that. Not much fun coming into an empty house – especially at night – but you do get used to it.'

'I cried my eyes out last night,' I admitted, but carefully left the impression that I had been on my own, and tried very hard not to think about what had followed after the tears, 'but I'm sure you're right and it will get easier. Stripping the bed gave me something to concentrate on and I always sleep better when the sheets have just been changed.'

I looked at my mother, sitting opposite me, neatly dressed, as she always was, not a grey hair on her head out of place and I felt a new respect for her. She always seemed so calm and coping, yet she must have had her times when life seemed almost too much to bear and I found myself saying as much.

'I find keeping busy is always the answer,' she said with a brisk nod, adding reprovingly, 'though I draw the line at changing beds late at night. No point sitting around feeling sorry for myself, is there? After all, I'm not the only widow in the world and your father would have expected me to get on with life. We were lucky to have a long and happy marriage and were blessed to have you and then Megan.'

'I'm afraid I've been a disappointment to you. You know, rushing off to get married, and then arriving back home with a child in tow when it didn't work out.' It was something I'd been meaning to say for a very long time, but I could never quite find the words before that moment, or prepare myself for the answer I might get.

'Nonsense,' my mother denied, pointing out, 'we both realized that neither children nor relationships come with a guarantee. Your dad and I were only too glad to be able to help out, though we were secretly hoping the split was only a temporary thing and that you and Charles would get back together once you'd sorted yourselves out.' I thought she looked wistful, but then she seemed to pull herself together. 'We did both really admire how you coped as a single mother,' she said briskly, 'setting up a home, and managing to run a business with a small child. Though, looking back, I could have hoped that you and Charles would have pulled together more after the separation, for Megan's sake.'

'I wish we had, too,' I said and I could see that I'd surprised her. 'I'm ashamed to admit that you could almost believe that Megan was the adult of the family and we were the children. I'm always amazed at how well she's turned out – in spite of her parents.'

'Well, I'll be the first one to say you are a very good mum and Charles has been a lovely dad. Megan hasn't wanted for anything and not many children from broken homes can say that. What did Charles want the other day?' she asked suddenly.

I almost jumped because the question was so unexpected. I had completely forgotten I'd spoken to my mother about the message he'd originally sent through Megan.

'When was that?' I feigned ignorance, stalling for time as I decided whether or not to tell my mother what was really going on. In the end I went for a watered-down version of the truth, because caught on the hop, it was all

I could come up with. 'Oh, yes,' I said. 'It was about some paperwork that was missing.'

I should have known that someone as sharp as my mother wasn't going to be satisfied with that.

'Paperwork, what paperwork?' she demanded. 'You haven't even seen each other for years, so why would he be asking you about paperwork?'

I could have kicked myself, and I thrashed around for a bit, looking for an answer that would satisfy her. Then I just gave in and decided to tell the truth.

'It's the decree absolute from our divorce. It seems to be missing. Do you fancy going out for a bit of lunch?' I added the last bit as a distraction and luckily it seemed to work.

'That would be nice,' she agreed immediately, so I grabbed my jacket and hurried her out of the house muttering something about beating the lunchtime rush.

I let my mother choose where we lunched and was surprised when she chose a golf club just outside town, though the Dudsbury had a reputation for fine food, attentive staff and a fabulous view of the surrounding countryside. I had actually been there with Martin once or twice but I wondered what had made my mother decide on that particular venue.

'Have you been here before?' I queried as I drove into the car park and slipped into a space between a top of the range Mercedes and a sleek Jaguar.

'Oh, yes, I come here with my friend Joan from time to time. I've even had a few lessons with some borrowed clubs,' she confided, adding with a little laugh, 'but I wasn't very good.'

I was impressed. 'Mum, that's great. You've never said anything.'

'Well, I don't tell you *everything*, dear, any more than you tell me everything.'

She wasn't even looking at me, as we walked arm in arm across the car park, but I felt as if she knew exactly what Chay and I had been up to the night before. I knew that it was ridiculous but couldn't quite dismiss the uncomfortable feeling the thought gave me.

'Will we get in, do you think?' I said adroitly changing the subject.

'Oh, I would think so. It's a bit early for the members yet. They seem to like a lie-in or a round of golf before Sunday lunch. I like it here,' she added as we went inside, 'it's so plush.'

I knew exactly what she meant. More used to cheap and cheerful, I'd been greatly impressed by such salubrious surroundings on my previous visits, and refused to worry about what lunch here might cost. I was really glad we had come and was already looking forward to my meal despite the toast I'd eaten only a short time ago. My enthusiasm lasted just until we set foot in the restaurant upstairs.

We had barely ascertained that they could fit us in, before my mother exclaimed, 'Oh, look there's Charles,' and took off between the tables, keeping a firm grip on my arm so that I had little choice but to go with her or face an embarrassing struggle to free myself.

'Ann,' Chay stood up immediately, looking delighted to see her – to see us both if I was honest – though the same couldn't be said of his extremely beautiful companion. Had she looked down her nose any further her heavily made-up eyes would have been completely crossed. 'And Tessa – why don't you both join us?'

I was swift with my refusal but Millicent was even quicker, flicking back her black hair and rushing to remind Chay, 'We were actually just about to leave, weren't we?' in the sort of tone I'd often used on Megan when she was small and I wanted her to remember her manners.

'Were we?' Chay looked at Millicent and then at his half-eaten meal in astonishment.

'Yes, I have a headache coming on.'

'Oh, you poor dear.' My mother was immediately all concern. 'I can offer you paracetamol.' She rummaged in her bag and managed to request a jug of water from a passing waiter at the same time. I couldn't believe she hadn't noticed an atmosphere you could have cut with a blunt knife.

'Come along, *Mother*.' I pulled on her arm and, ignoring Chay, told Millicent, 'We'll leave you to finish your lunch in peace.'

For the briefest moment I thought I was going to get my own way and no harm would be done, because my mother had even moved a step or two away from the table; then she stopped and, before I could do anything to prevent it, my mother said clearly, 'What's this about some decree that's been lost, Charles? Tessa was just telling me about it. What exactly does that mean?'

'Yes, Ann, that's exactly what I would like to know.' The change in Millicent was instantaneous; going from uninterested to the point of rude, she was now actively encouraging my mother to sit down and join them.

My first instinct was to walk away, dragging my mother with me if I had to. After all, what did Chay's and my decree absolute have to do with bloody Millicent? To be fair, though – and I found myself cursing that part of me that seemed programmed to be fair – if she was keen to marry my ex, and the lack of a decree was the only thing stopping her, it did have everything to do with her.

'We won't join you, if you don't mind,' I said, so firmly that my mother ignored the chair that had been pulled out for her and remained by my side. 'The problem with the decree is one that will be easily resolved once I have tracked down the solicitor who acted for me, and obtained a copy.'

'So, you did have the decree, but you lost it.' Millicent somehow managed to glare at me through narrowed eyes. 'Is that what you are saying?' She sounded as if she were questioning a small child and I came very close to losing it with her.

'Do you know what, Millie?' I said nastily, 'I don't remember, because at the time I was too busy bringing up our young child, making a home for us both, and starting up a business to be bothered about something that was a mere detail. As far as I'm concerned, Chay – Charles – and I are divorced and you can safely start planning your wedding. Now our daughter is safely settled at university, you can be sure I will make chasing the paperwork that proves the marriage is over my priority. Enjoy what's left of your lunch.'

I spun on my heel and, with my mother following meekly behind me, made for a table on the far side of the restaurant.

'Bravo, dear.' The note of approval in the soft voice was much appreciated, as was the gentle hand on mine. I only realized then that I was actually shaking.

My mother ordered wine for us both very competently, also requesting a jug of water for the table, giving me time to calm down. From the corner of my eye I saw Millicent and Chay leave the restaurant. I breathed an imperceptible sigh of relief.

'Did you. . . ?'

'Know that they came here?' my mother finished. 'No, I didn't, or I probably wouldn't have suggested coming. Although,' she added, 'I thought Megan said you were getting along better these days.'

'Ish,' was all I said, and left it at that.

'I'm very fond of Charles,' my mother said, 'but I can't say I'm impressed with that woman. Mutton dressed as lamb, if you ask me,' she added with a disdainful sniff.

After feeling not only my age, but downright dowdy next to the smartly dressed and immaculately made up Millicent, there was nothing my mother could have said that was more likely to put a smile back on my face.

We went off to the carvery, filling our plates from the delicious choice of meat and vegetables, though in my case I didn't seriously think I would be able to eat a thing.

'A sip of wine won't hurt you,' my mother pointed out, 'and it might relax you a bit.'

She was right of course, as she usually was, and we both tucked in with relish, appreciating a meal beautifully prepared and cooked by someone else. We even managed a pudding afterwards.

'So,' she said, when she had scraped the bowl clean and licked the spoon – trifle had always been a favourite of hers, 'what's the problem with this piece of paper?'

I told my mother the whole story, leaving nothing out.

'Do you think you ever had this decree in the first place?'

I shrugged. 'I really don't know, Mum. It's all so long ago, and so much has happened. My solicitor should have applied for the decree absolute, as far as I am aware, and probably he did, but unless I can find him it will be hard to prove. According to Charlie, when he tried to get a copy – presumably from the court – he was told the divorce was never finalized.'

'So what does that mean exactly, dear?' She was looking at me closely.

'Well,' I began, reluctant to say the words out loud.

'Yes?' She pressed for an answer.

'Well,' I pulled a face and then said in a rush, 'we could still be married.'

'Oh.' My mother turned quickly to order coffee from a waiter, but not before I had seen her expression.

I could hardly believe it, tried to tell myself I was wrong, but there was really no doubt about that tiny smile. Could my mother really be *pleased* that Chay and I were still husband and wife?

CHAPTER NINE

Despite my mother's strange behaviour in the restaurant, she did eventually prove very helpful – although in the process she made me feel more than a little stupid for not thinking of doing it myself first.

'What about the Internet, dear? I do find Google very helpful for most things.'

'So, you're a silver-surfer, are you? Megan seemed to think you might be.' I couldn't help smiling in spite of my astonishment and I was impressed.

'Well, there is all that information at your fingertips. If that law firm still exists they'll be bound to have a website. I'm surprised you don't make more use of yours, dear.'

'It was enough hassle getting the thing set up in the first place and I can't say it's made a huge difference to my life or to my business. I get more than enough in the way of dressmaking and alterations to keep me busy through word of mouth,' I reminded her a little shortly and not altogether truthfully since a percentage of my business did come via the website. 'I use my computer for my accounts and that's about it. You can get completely drawn in and waste far too much time on various sites if you're not careful.'

'I know.' My mother nodded sagely. 'I already have around two hundred friends on Facebook, but I do draw the line at twittering or whatever it's called.'

I suddenly became aware that my mouth was hanging open, and snapped it shut in a hurry. 'You're already on Face. . . ?' I stuttered. 'But Megan only just said you were thinking about it. How on earth did you know what to do?'

We were driving home at the time and I had to force myself to concentrate on the road ahead and not stare at my mother in absolute awe.

'Mmm,' she said. 'I learned the basic use of a computer at the adult learning centre – there were a lot of people my age there, and then our Megan and Tom kindly gave me a few pointers. I found it quite easy to register and then I was off. Well,' she admitted, 'I have more time on my hands than you do. Shall I look up the name of the company for you?'

'I think I can manage,' I said drily, bringing the car to a halt outside her neat little terrace house. 'You be careful who you get talking to on line, mind. People aren't always who they say they are, and a lot of people end up being fleeced out of their life savings by unscrupulous characters pretending to be something they're not.'

'Old people like me, you mean?' She turned in her seat to give me a very straight look, before adding, 'I'm not stupid, you know. My contacts are mostly old school chums and neighbours from years ago. I don't accept anyone I'm not sure of. Cup of tea?'

'I won't, if you don't mind. Now you've got me through most of the first day, I think I can face the empty house, and I want to get myself organized for tomorrow. I've really neglected my business these last couple of weeks and the orders are piling up.'

'Don't work twenty-four hours a day, now,' my mother warned, wagging a finger at me. 'You know what they say about all work and no play. What about that young man you were seeing?'

I realized with a shock that I hadn't given him a single thought since we'd spoken the day before. A lot had happened since then and, in view of what had so recently happened with Chay, it also seemed a bit dishonest to be contemplating a weekend away with Martin. I'd never been the sort of girl – or woman, come to that – who slept around.

I didn't think I was blushing, but it would hardly have been surprising if I was, as I said in a careless tone, 'Oh, yes, Martin. I had a drink with him last week and spoke to him briefly on the phone yesterday.'

'Megan told me he's very good-looking.' Thankfully, my mother wasn't looking at me as she rummaged in her handbag for the door key.

I wondered what else Megan had told her, because she had never been Martin's biggest fan, but I simply said, 'He is – very.'

'And is he nice with it?' Her grey gaze rested on my face.

'Of course,' I replied quickly, probably a bit too quickly.

'It would be lovely to see you settled with someone again.' My mother patted my cheek. 'You're far too young to be on your own and you deserve to be happy.'

'I am. . . .' I began.

'You know what I mean,' she said. She reached for the door handle and climbed out on to the pavement. 'Take care, dear, and remember, don't work too hard.'

Easier said than done, I discovered when I arrived home and hurried upstairs to my sewing room, switching lights on as I went and trying my best to ignore the empty rooms and the silence. If I had been looking for a distraction I was in the right place. Looking round at the half finished garments and the bulging order book I had to fight down a feeling of panic that was completely foreign to me.

I had built my whole reputation on reliability. My customers knew with certainty that they could safely leave their orders for that special occasion in my capable hands, knowing the outfit would be ready and waiting in good time, allowing for any minor alterations. It had been madness just to leave it all, but with Megan going away and needing my support, what else could I have done?

I took a few deep breaths and then began to prioritize, so that work with an imminent deadline would be taken care of first. That done, I allowed myself a cup of tea before I set to work and, once I had started, I just kept going. One of the previously unrealized benefits of living alone was that I could work through the night if I chose without disturbing anyone. By the time the sun made an appearance the most urgent orders were on hangers, pressed and ready for a final fitting.

Feeling pleased with myself as I climbed exhausted into bed, I decided I would keep up the momentum and work all the hours I could manage until I was back on track. I refused to think about Martin and the weekend. I definitely wasn't going to waste any of my precious time thinking about Chay and giving any importance to what happened between us. He had caught me at a vulnerable moment, that was all, and it didn't mean a thing.

My days had no real beginning and no natural end, as I worked when I woke – whatever that time was – ate when I was hungry and slept when I was exhausted. I had the satisfaction of seeing the majority of orders completed and ready for collection in a matter of days.

I was shocked when a phone call from Martin reminded me that it was already Thursday evening and our weekend away was imminent. He sounded so unlike his usual self, pleased and almost excited, and making it so clear that he couldn't wait to see me that I just didn't have it in me to burst his bubble and make any of the excuses that popped into my head. Cursing myself for a coward when he rang off – after reminding me to be ready to be picked up around 7.30 the following evening – I found it was easier to throw myself into my work again and continue to try to ignore the whole thing.

I did take time to wonder though, as I sewed intricate beading to a bodice by hand, whether Martin might have booked separate rooms for us. Then I almost laughed out loud at my own naïvety as I recalled the raw promise in his tone before he put the phone down, reminding myself that we were two consenting adults who had been seeing each other for quite a while and a physical relationship would obviously be the next natural step to take.

I also tried to convince myself that the fact that I had slept with someone else recently probably wouldn't even be a problem for Martin; after all he had never given me the impression until very recently that our relationship might be exclusive or even anything very serious.

Somehow, though, I just knew I was fooling myself. I couldn't see someone like Martin sharing the affections of the lady in his life – but that was really the whole point, I thought – was I *the* lady in his life or just one of many? Perhaps it would be as well to get a few things established before our relationship became more intimate.

And what about Chay? I wondered, then got really cross with myself and fumed, Well, what about bloody Chay? I stabbed the needle with more force than was

99

necessary and found myself sucking the blood from yet another pricked finger, careful to keep it away from the beaded material. What had happened between us was meaningless, a mistake pure and simple. It was just as I had said, a moment of madness that would never be repeated and was best forgotten.

Well, he obviously thought so, since there had been not so much as a whisper from his direction all week, and part of me – a very unreasonable part, I was forced to remind myself – was quite disgruntled about the lack of contact. I wasn't sure exactly what I had been expecting, but it had been *something*, and I felt very let down and very stupid for feeling that way. How fickle was I? I had absolutely no interest in Chay and would have been horrified to think he was still interested in me. The very last thing I wanted was to find two men vying for my affections.

Making a determined effort to put the whole thing out of my mind, I went to bed at a relatively early hour, slept like the proverbial baby, and woke refreshed. I had kept the day sewing free for a few customer appointments and for packing my weekend bag, though every time I walked past the bedroom my stomach turned over at the sight of it sitting unzipped and open on the bed. I realized that I had absolutely no idea what to pack.

I dithered between sensible pyjamas – though they *were* silk – or the strappy nightdress Megan had bought me last Christmas, which had never been worn. Cotton underwear – bought for comfort rather than seduction –

sat in little piles. I shivered, then went hot at the thought of Martin and me getting so up close and personal that he would attempt to remove it. We'd never done much more than kiss and a whole weekend away suddenly seemed pretty daunting.

I didn't know what was wrong with me. It wasn't so long ago that I had been amazed and delighted that someone like Martin would give someone like me the time of day. It was quite obvious that, when it came to women, Martin could take his pick. You wouldn't have thought a single mother heading for forty would be high on his wish list and certainly, to begin with, I hadn't got the impression that I was. In fact, I spent a lot of time wondering why he was seeing me at all – when he bothered that was, because he often broke more dates than he kept.

Somewhere along the way there seemed to have been a change of heart for both of us and, as I had become a little less interested, Martin appeared to have suddenly decided I was worth spending time with. I wondered if that was a coincidence. Perhaps playing hard to get really was the way to go.

With the confused state of mind I was already in, finding Chay standing on my step late in the afternoon was a complication I could well do without.

'What do *you* want?' I said, sounding churlish even to my own ears.

He didn't look at all put out – far from it. 'Is that any way to greet your husband?'

101

'*Ex*,' I snapped, holding the door half-closed, and standing in the gap just in case Chay had any ideas about inviting himself in.

'As we both know,' he reminded, '*that* has yet to be proved.'

'And as soon as I get a minute,' I assured him, 'it will be.'

He laughed, actually laughed, and said, 'If you're so keen to be rid of me, I'd have thought you'd be making it your absolute priority.'

'I've been a bit busy,' I said lamely, adding quickly and belligerently, 'I do have customers, you know, and *they* pay my bills, not you, so they have to come first.'

Right on cue one of my favourite clients came through the gate.

'I'll keep you posted on any progress by email,' I said tersely to Chay before greeting the smiling lady, 'Mrs Etteridge, do come in. I'm all ready for you. This is Charles, he was just leaving.'

I opened the door wider to usher her in and before I knew what was happening Chay had slipped though the gap.

'I'm in no hurry,' he told us both and making his way to the kitchen, advised, 'I'll go and put the kettle on.'

'Who is *that*, dear?' the elderly lady's blue eyes were bright with curiosity. 'Did you find him on the Internet?'

I shook my head, wondering if she was another silver-surfer, and just refrained from adding that if I had I would have deleted him pretty smartly.

'He seems very nice.'

'Mmm.' I was carefully non-committal and again stopped myself from saying that was a matter of opinion as I led the way upstairs.

One of my best customers, with her three cruises a year, Mrs Etteridge adored wearing something to make a statement and together we came up with the goods every time. Despite her age, at which I stabbed a guess of late seventies, early eighties, she carried herself well and had obviously been a real beauty in her time.

Smoothing the material of the deep-blue floor-length gown over enviably slim hips, she nodded, turning this way and that in front of the mirror.

'I know I should probably be dressing more sedately to suit my advancing years, but black and grey are so *ageing*, dear, and I fell out of love with pleats years ago.'

'You look gorgeous,' I said, and I meant it. I would never let a customer of mine leave with something that didn't do them justice.

'I wish Madge thought so.' Mrs Etteridge sighed, and shook her head. 'Sisters we might be but we've never been a bit alike and she's so critical of my choices.'

'Perhaps she's a little bit jealous?' I suggested gently, speaking as I felt, but not wishing to overstep the mark. 'You always look so stunning. Are you alike?'

Mrs Ettridge shook her head. Her hair was snow-white as befitted her age, but it was short and spiked – a style that, in my experience, you didn't often find in ladies of advanced years, yet it suited her admirably.

'I find her dull and she thinks I'm outrageous. I do wish I could persuade her to pay you a visit. I'm sure you could do something to liven up her image.'

As we came down the stairs Chay appeared in the kitchen doorway. 'Can I offer you a cup of tea, Mrs Etteridge?'

'Well, how nice of you to offer,' she twinkled, 'but sadly, I must refuse because I have a boat to catch. He's *lovely*,' she said in a stage whisper that Chay couldn't have missed hearing. 'You don't want to let him get away.'

I didn't have the heart to tell her that I'd let him get away years ago and that I really didn't want him back.

'What do you want, Chay?' I said wearily, sitting down and reaching for the cup of tea he poured for me, and refusing a biscuit. 'I don't know what you're doing here, but please just say what you came to say and go. I'm going away for the weekend, in case you've forgotten, and I still haven't finished packing.'

He looked shocked for a minute and I knew he *had* forgotten.

'You're not still going, are you?' he demanded, sitting up straight in his chair.

I stared at him. 'Yes, I am as it happens, though what it has to do with you what I do, where I go, or whom I see, I have no idea.'

'But – after what happened between us?'

'What did happen?' I looked him right in the eye. 'When it comes down to it, Chay, what did really happen? It was stupid, pointless, and meaningless. It shouldn't have happened, and it won't happen again – not ever.'

He leaned towards me. 'How can you be so sure of that?'

'We can't turn back time, Chay. Go home to your girlfriend, fiancée, whatever she is, and plan your wedding – and this time, try to make it work.'

CHAPTER TEN

Chay looked as if I had slapped him, hard, then he got up from the table and left without another word, closing the front door quietly behind him.

I refused to regret my words because, harsh though they might have been, they were nothing but the truth. I wasn't entirely sure what had happened between us that night, or how we had ended up making love, but I did know it was all wrong and we shouldn't have allowed ourselves to get carried away. There was no excuse; we weren't silly kids any more and should have had more control.

That said, I refused to dwell on it for a moment longer and went to pack with more determination than I had shown all day. If I had any concerns about this weekend with Martin and what might or might not happen between us, I pushed them to the back of my mind. The small case was packed and standing by the door and I was showered, dressed, and ready to leave when the phone rang.

'Martin?' I said, at the sound of his voice, 'Where are you?'

'Darling,' he said, 'I really am so *dreadfully* sorry but the weekend's off. All hell has just broken loose here, something that has obviously been looming for some time but been kept from us has now been dumped – pretty literally – in our laps. It's all hands to the pumps if we're to avoid disaster. It's not just my job on the line; the whole company could go under. None of us will be going home tonight. You do understand?'

Martin had broken dates before, often at the last minute, but this time I believed he was speaking the truth. He sounded tired, upset and regretful.

'It's fine,' I told him firmly. 'Just do what you have to do. Your job is your whole future and that's far more important than a couple of days that can very easily be rescheduled.'

'I don't deserve your understanding, or you, come to that. I've come to realize that recently – a little late in the day, I know – but I will make this up to you, Tessa.'

It was only after I had unpacked and was sitting in front of the TV in my comfy slippers and cosy fleece dressing-gown, sipping a mug of hot chocolate, that I realized that my overwhelming feeling wasn't one of disappointment, but relief.

Perhaps I wasn't ready for a grown-up relationship yet – with anyone. After all, the daughter I had always put first had only just flown the nest and my new-found freedom still felt strange. For the first time in the whole of my adult life there was only me to consider and perhaps I should learn to enjoy pleasing myself for a little while before contemplating any kind of involvement with the opposite sex.

With that thought I felt as if a huge weight had been lifted from my shoulders and I settled back to enjoy a soap fest – watching several episodes of the various popular programmes without fear of anyone snatching the remote away or playing music upstairs loud enough to make following dialogue and storylines difficult, if not impossible.

I didn't expect to stop missing Meggie and her bright company overnight, but a determined effort to enjoy some of the undoubted benefits of living alone made me view things from a different and more positive perspective. I went to bed feeling relaxed and quite philosophical about a future that was all mine to do with as I pleased.

A good night's sleep helped to keep the mellow mood going. I started the day with a check list of the orders not yet completed – exactly where I stood with each one and how close the completion date was, which convinced me that there was no need to fill up the unexpected free time by rushing back to work.

Opening the door to Megan's room was a big step, but remembering the mess inside I knew I couldn't keep it closed up for ever. After I had turned the mattress and picked up the items of clothing left scattered far and wide, I set to with the duster and polish and then vacuumed. With the bed made up with fresh linen the room had a pristine look I'd never managed to achieve for long when my daughter was at home, but it looked welcoming – ready for when she came home again.

The phone rang as I came in from pegging out the washing.

'Oh.' It was Megan. 'I was about to hang up when I realized I'd rung the home phone by mistake. I thought Dad said you were away for the weekend and I was ringing to see how it was going. What happened?'

'There's some sort of crisis at Martin's firm.'

I didn't get a chance to say any more than that, as Megan fumed, 'For God's sake, Mum, he's *always* letting you down. I don't know why you put up with him; you're worth better.'

'It's fine, honestly. I'm not a bit bothered and I did believe him, as it happens.'

The doorbell rang and I went to answer it with the phone still pressed to my ear, listening to Megan telling me, quite bluntly, what she would like to do to Martin if she got hold of him.

Flowers filled the doorway and a voice from behind them asked, 'Ms Wallis?' and when I agreed, continued, 'These are for you.'

'What is it, what's happening?' Megan demanded.

'I think Kew Gardens just got delivered,' I told her with a shaky laugh as I struggled to manhandle the arrangement through to the kitchen, where I placed it on the table and stepped back to admire the biggest bouquet I had ever seen – much less received.

'Flowers? Who from?'

'I think I just got a huge apology for missing out on a weekend away,' I said, studying the printed card.

'Humph. Well, at least he did that much.' Megan sounded as if she might have mellowed slightly. 'That's a first.'

'I've decided I need time on my own anyway. I don't think I'm ready for a relationship yet, and certainly not a serious one.'

'But you've been on your own for years, Mum,' she protested.

'Don't make it sound as if I've been on the shelf all this time, Megan,' I admonished. 'I've had my moments, however few and far between they might have been, and I've never really been alone, have I, because I've always had you? And, much as I love you, I want to spend some time right now pleasing myself, watching sloppy films when I'm not working, enjoying my kind of music, getting up when I like and going to bed when I'm tired.'

'Don't you get too used to it,' Megan warned, in a stern tone, 'because I will be back before you know it.'

'And it will be wonderful to have you here. How is it going, anyway? I want to hear all about it.'

I sat in the chair, admiring my flowers and listening to my daughter extolling the wonders of the midwifery course she had only just embarked on. I couldn't be anything other than thrilled to hear her sounding so happy and enthusiastic.

I put the phone down in an even better frame of mind than before. Megan was clearly getting on with her life and it was time I got on with mine. Unfortunately, I lacked the one thing that my daughter had in abundance – and that was the assortment of friends that was a requirement of a good social life. Working from home for so many years and allowing myself to become totally wrapped up in my daughter did have its drawbacks in that way. However, it was no good bemoaning the lack if I wasn't prepared to get off my behind and do something about meeting new people. The pity was that I had no idea where to start, so I boiled the kettle to make myself a cup of coffee while I thought about it.

I looked at the flowers, beautifully arranged and already in water, and then I looked at the list I had made of my dressmaking orders and reached for the pen. I would make a list of all the different ways I could think of for meeting people. Evening classes was one of them – though perhaps *not* flower-arranging.

I couldn't actually think of anything else but that seemed as good a place to start as anything else I might come up with so, as I was eager not to waste another minute, the coffee was poured down the sink and off I went. It was actually a pleasant day for early October with a weak but warm sun convincing me that the route through the local park to the library was appealing.

I couldn't remember the last time I had taken time off on a Saturday simply for leisure. Shopping with Megan, yes, often; a trip to buy material or pick out patterns, yes, regularly, but this felt as if I was playing truant. There was a real spring in my step as I walked past a pond with the ducks crowding the edges to eagerly snap up crusts of bread being tossed to them.

'Tessa? It is Tessa, isn't it?'

I stared blankly at the lady walking towards me with a small black dog pulling on its leash beside her.

'Jean, Jean Watson,' she reminded me with a smile as we got closer, 'from three doors down. Unusual to see you out and about without your daughter. Not ill, is she?'

'Gone away to university,' I explained, adding with none of my usual reticence, 'leaving me with time on my hands for once. I was just going to the library to pick up some information on courses.'

'You'll be lucky,' she said, ordering the dog to 'sit' now that we were facing each other. 'They only open for a short time on Saturdays now – or any other day for that matter. Cutbacks, you know.'

'Oh.' I felt quite deflated, having psyched myself up to do something about my social life – or lack of one – without delay, even if it was only picking up an adult learners brochure.

'Was it something in particular you were looking for?'

'Something to get me out of the house,' I found myself admitting in a burst of honesty. 'Never mind, another time will do. I might just as well walk back with you now if you're going that way.'

As we fell into step she asked in a friendly way, 'You work from home, don't you?' I nodded, and she continued, 'It sounds wonderful on a rainy day, but I suppose the drawback is not getting out to meet people other than your customers. I'm retired now, so I had much the same problem, but getting the dog solved that for me. He gets me out, don't you, Ben? And I've made lots of friends among the other dog-walkers. Always someone to chat to in the park.'

'Oh, I don't think a dog is for me,' I said, thinking about muddy paws and hairs on my customers' garments.

'No, I realize they're not for everyone. You are very tied with a dog, and they have to be walked, rain or shine, but they are great company. Ben is a big improvement on my late husband.' Jean clapped a hand over her mouth but it didn't hide the fact that she was smiling as she murmured, 'For one thing, he never answers back.'

We both laughed, and stopped as we reached Jean's gate.

'It's been really nice talking to you,' I said, and found to my surprise that I meant it. I'd never been one for chatting – always in too much of a hurry, I guessed.

'Why don't you come in for five minutes?' Jean offered, opening the gate in a gesture of welcome. 'Go on, just a quick cup of tea, and then you can get back to your work. Dressmaking, isn't it? I've often been tempted to knock your door, especially when I can't find what I want in the shops.'

113

Without noticing how I got there, I found myself standing next to Jean as she slid the key in the door. The next minute I was ushered inside a house structurally identical to my own, though that was where any similarity ended. There was no other word for it – the place gleamed. From the parquet flooring under my feet, to the banisters edging the stairs and every surface as far as the eye could see, everything shone.

I had always done my best, even though housework wasn't my favourite pastime – and been relatively satisfied with the results – but Jean's home made mine look like a complete hovel by comparison. I wished I hadn't come inside, because I knew there was no way I would be returning the invitation.

'Come on through,' she said cheerily, seemingly unaware of my awe.

I went warily, wondering that the dog seemed to have the run of the house. I wouldn't have been surprised to find him relegated to a kennel in the garden, but he trotted happily across a tiled floor I'd have happily eaten my dinner from and settled into a dog bed in the corner of the kitchen.

Eventually Jean must have noticed something about the way I was looking round. 'What is it?' she asked as she filled her shiny kettle from an even shinier tap. 'Something wrong?'

I couldn't help it, I just blurted it out, 'Your house is so *clean* – not that I expected it to be dirty, but. . . .' I tailed off, not really knowing what else to say.

114

'I'm not house-proud,' Jean said hastily, 'it's just that, even with the dog to walk, I have far too much time on my hands and not too much money to burn. There are only so many hours in a day you can spend reading or watching TV, and I do actually enjoy cleaning. Come to think of it, perhaps joining a class is something I should be thinking about.'

'You won't need dog obedience classes,' I pointed out, nodding to where Ben was curled up in his bed. 'He's very well behaved.'

'Isn't he?' she agreed proudly. 'I never worry about leaving him on his own for an hour or so. Not that I go out very much, these days. I got out of the habit when Gerald – my late husband – became ill.'

'Perhaps we could go out together sometimes?' I said rashly. 'You know, for a meal, or even just a glass of wine.'

Jean's face lit up – there was no other word for the sudden change in her expression. 'Oh,' she said, 'that would be lovely.'

'Tonight?'

'But where would we go,' she asked, 'and what on earth would I wear?'

'What you have on is fine,' I assured her. 'I was only thinking of the local pub. They do very nice meals – at a reasonable price,' I added hastily recalling her comment about not having money to burn.

I think we were both almost excited at the thought of a night out, and a meal cooked by someone other than ourselves, eaten while enjoying a chat with someone like-

115

minded. I was smiling and the spring was back in my step as I walked the few steps to my own front door. I couldn't believe how quick and easy it had been to make a new friend.

'Tessa.'

I whirled round to find Chay standing right behind me. I hadn't even heard his footsteps on the path.

'Jesus, Cha – rlie, you frightened me half to death, creeping up on me like that. What the hell are you playing at? What do you want?'

'Um, well, actually, I spoke to Megan earlier and she seemed to think you might be at a loose end. Just wondered if you fancied going out this evening, you know, for a meal or a show?'

I beamed at him. I could actually feel my face breaking into a big smile, as I assured him. 'Sorry, Charlie, but I've already made plans.'

'But Megan said—'

'That the weekend away was off, no doubt. Well, for one thing, she shouldn't be discussing my social calendar with you, and two, as I'm not one to let the grass grow under my feet, I have already made other arrangements. Thank you for the offer, but no thanks.'

I skipped through the door, closing it behind me in Chay's surprised face. I leaned back against the door, amused for a moment and then furious as I reminded myself that his interest in me wasn't at all appropriate. I was willing to bet that Millicent wouldn't be amused if she discovered he was sniffing around his ex – well, soon to be – ex-wife. The sooner that divorce was finalized, the better things would be all round.

CHAPTER ELEVEN

I jumped again when the phone rang and snatched it up, half expecting to hear Chay's voice, but it was Martin, very sweet and apologetic, and hoping I had liked the flowers.

'They're gorgeous. Thank you so much,' I said warmly, 'but you shouldn't have worried. You obviously have a lot on your mind right now.'

'Well, I'm more hopeful than I was that disaster may be avoided in the end, in which case it will have been worth all the effort. It's been a real team effort. We're all looking the worse for wear from the hours we've put in, and it will be a while longer before we know for sure how things will turn out, but at least we've tried.' The words came from a slightly humbler Martin than the man I had come to know, who had always seemed to have things easy in his life – and to take the trappings of success for granted.

'Well, that's wonderful,' I said, and meant it.

'But what about you?' he asked. 'A wasted weekend for

you, I'm afraid. I hope you haven't been working all day. I know what you're like. And what's it to be tonight – feet up in front of the TV?'

'Actually, no, I'm going out for a meal.'

'Oh?' Martin's concerned tone changed to one of suspicion in a minute. I could hear it clearly. He didn't sound pleased, or very happy either. 'Who with?'

I almost said, *none of your business*, but it seemed a bit harsh, given that he hadn't let me down on purpose. I wouldn't tell an outright lie but in the end I compromised with a careless, 'Just a friend,' and hurried on, 'so you see, you needn't worry about me. I shall be fine and won't be sitting at home twiddling my thumbs at all. Thank you for ringing and for the wonderful flowers. I look forward to hearing soon that everything has turned out as you hoped.'

Settling the phone firmly on its stand, I mused that it must have been one of the very few times that I had ended a call to Martin instead of the other way round.

It actually felt really nice to be getting ready for a night out that didn't involve making the extra effort that always seemed to be required when it was a date. I felt quite relaxed and anticipated a nice chatty evening of the kind that Megan and I had often enjoyed, and I was right.

We talked about clothes.

'You do look nice in those jeans,' Jean said enviously. 'I suppose I'm too old to wear something like that?'

'Nonsense,' I assured her, guessing she was about fifteen or twenty years older than me but looking great

119

for her age. 'Jeans are for everyone and with your lovely slim figure you would look great in a pair. Boot cut would probably suit you best, and a nice pair of boots with a little heel.'

We discussed my work and the kind of garments I was asked to make.

'Anything from christening to wedding gowns, fancy dress to a plain shift dress – and I do love a challenge.'

We talked about her years working in local government and the sort of people she worked with – from charming and grateful for her knowledge and expertise, to extremely rude and full of arrogance.

She touched on life as a widow, and I shared something of my life as a single mother.

We were both amazed at the end of the evening to find we had consumed everything on the plates we had piled high from the selection at the carvery, followed by the puddings of our choice, and imbibing two glasses of Pinot Grigio apiece into the bargain.

'Well,' Jean said happily as we settled the very reasonable bill between us, 'I don't know when I've spent a nicer evening. Certainly not for a very long time.'

'It has been lovely, hasn't it? I'd forgotten how enjoyable a mature girls' night out could be.'

'I hope we can do it again sometime.' Jean looked at me hopefully as we slipped into our jackets and made our way outside. 'When you have time, of course. I know how busy you are, while I'm the one with too much time on my hands.'

'Well, I've had a thought about that,' I linked my arm through hers, 'and I wondered—' I hesitated and then ploughed on— 'If you would consider doing my cleaning, but only if you really do enjoy it? I would pay you the going rate, of course.'

'Do you know, I'd actually been thinking along similar lines.' She stopped and turned me round to face her, there in the street. 'I would be happy to do it for the occasional outfit if you think we could come to some agreement. I wouldn't be wanting anything too flash.'

'We'll work something out,' I promised as we set off again. 'And don't forget we're going shopping for those jeans you've been longing to try.'

I couldn't help reflecting again as I fell asleep that night that making my first female friend for years had taken very little effort at all. I also reached the sleepy conclusion that life seemed to be so much simpler when men were not involved.

I woke, feeling rested and in good humour, to a second Sunday that wasn't all planned out. I refused to get out of bed immediately or to even think about working. Tomorrow was as good a time as any to get back to a routine and what would pass as my normal life from now on and, to my surprise, I found that I was quite looking forward to it. Though I hated to admit it, I was already noticing that I had so much more time now that I wasn't running around after Megan. After dreading facing my empty nest for so long it actually wasn't anywhere near as bad as I'd feared once I'd got over the initial shock.

Leisurely was the word for my morning. I enjoyed scrambled egg on toast and several cups of tea while reading a Sunday paper that didn't have all the celebrity pages missing. I enjoyed showering with no one hammering on the bathroom door, spending time smoothing moisturizer into my skin, straightening my hair so that it fell sleek and shiny round my face, all without interruption. Then it all started to go horribly wrong.

I was actually on my way outside with the WD-40, intent on spraying some on to the hinges of the creaking gate after months of putting up with the irritating sound, when I came face to face with Martin coming up the garden path. If I had doubted his reasons for cancelling the weekend – which I honestly hadn't – I'd have had to revise my opinion, because he looked as if he hadn't slept for days. I had time to note that the rugged, unshaven look made quite a change from his usual polished appearance. It wasn't at all unattractive, but what surprised me was that I wasn't really all that pleased to have him arrived unannounced, despite the beautiful bouquet of flowers he was carrying.

'Martin,' I said, trying to inject some enthusiasm into my tone, 'what are you doing here?'

Handing me the flowers, he said, 'I wanted to surprise you and I know it's small consolation, but I thought perhaps we could go out to lunch somewhere special and salvage at least some of the weekend.'

'My sentiments exactly,' drawled an all too familiar

voice, and I spun round to find Chay leaning nonchalantly against the gatepost. 'But I didn't expect to find *you* here.' He glared at Martin. 'I was led to believe that you had baled out of the weekend you had planned.'

'Yes, unfortunately and unavoidably,' Martin said stiffly, in a what's-it-got-to-do-with-you-mate? kind of way. 'Tessa absolutely understood, didn't you, darling?'

The two men were almost bristling as they sized each other up, like two dogs spoiling for a fight. I wondered idly who would come off worse and then gave myself a mental shake and a sharp reminder not to be so childish.

'I'm sure she did.' Chay sneered. 'She's nothing if not understanding and she's probably used to having you cancel. I have it on good authority that you do exactly that at the last minute on a regular basis.'

I gasped, cursing Megan and her thoughtless tongue, because Chay could have got such personal information from no one else. I went to jump in to say that it was none of Chay's business what Martin and I did or didn't do.

Before I could say a word, Martin sneered, 'I only cancelled a weekend. I have it on good authority that you cancelled out a whole marriage and therefore gave up any right at all to comment on how your ex-wife spends her time – or who with.'

My gaze flew to Chay's face. I could absolutely tell by his furious expression that he was about to take the greatest pleasure in telling Martin – in no uncertain terms, just how much of an ex-wife I was. At that very moment Jean walked out of her house three doors down and provided me with the diversion I was so desperately looking for.

Ignoring the two men, I waved merrily, and called, 'Hi Jean. Still on for our shopping trip today, are you?'

To her absolute credit, after one brief startled look, she grasped the urgency of the situation in a moment. 'Wouldn't miss it for the world,' she stated with great enthusiasm and barely missing a beat. 'Just taking Ben for a quick walk and I'll be ready any time you are.'

'I'll just grab a coat and join you. I could do with a breath of fresh air.'

I was in the house, had grabbed a jacket, and was out again in seconds, slamming the door behind me. Shrugging into the jacket, I walked past the two men who were by now, speechless as they watched me go.

At the gate I paused and, smiling, said over my shoulder, 'As you can see, I've already made plans so, whatever yours might have been, I'm afraid they won't include me.'

Jean was full of it. 'What's going on there, then? They both look absolutely furious.'

I shook my head. 'You don't want to know, but thank you so much for bailing me out.'

She laughed. 'You're very welcome, but I might just hold you to the promise of a Sunday shopping trip, unless you have something else planned.'

'It's the very least I can do,' I assured her. I smiled all the way round the park at the thought of the look on the faces of the two men I had left standing in the middle of my path with the discarded can of WD-40 on the ground at their feet. Perhaps one of them might even think to give the squeaky hinge a quick spray before he left, saving me the job but, somehow, I doubted it.

There was no sign of them when we got back from the park, but the flowers and can had been left on my front doorstep. The gate no longer squealed when it was pushed open, I was gratified to note. I wondered idly which one had taken that little job upon himself and even if there had been a bit of a tussle over the can.

The shopping trip was a great success and I was encouraged to splash out on a couple of sweaters myself, just because someone else was there to tell me what suited me – or not, as the case might be.

Jean was thrilled with her jeans and the black boots she'd bought especially to go with them.

'Who'd have thought it, me, in denim?' She watched the assistant placing both items in bags with great glee. 'The late husband would have gone mad.'

'Well, I don't know why, because you have a great figure and look fabulous in them. Fancy lunch?'

I couldn't believe Jean had never eaten a panini or drunk a latte, because the late husband 'didn't like foreign muck' – or shopping either, it became apparent – and I wondered aloud at the amount of control men appeared to have over us.

'Over me, perhaps, for many years,' Jean said ruefully, 'but you seem to have it sussed. I'd never have dared walk away from my marriage and make a life of my own, or dream of leaving one man abandoned on my doorstep as you did today, never mind two.'

'Nor me.' I grinned, 'I don't know what's come over me – but I quite like it. The marriage, of course, I wasn't given a choice about ending, though looking back it was probably for the best.'

Jean started working her thorough magic on my house the very next day and I noticed a difference immediately. I left it up to her to decide on the hours she worked to begin with, though I kept a note of them, feeling sure she would undercut herself. It was quite obvious my slapdash housekeeping was nowhere near to meeting her high standards, so it would take a while for her to settle into any sort of routine.

I felt she couldn't have come along at a better time for several reasons, one of them being that I had been turning clients away for quite some time, often using the excuse that I had Megan living at home and that she needed me more than I needed the extra money. Now I no longer had that excuse or the housework to hinder me. The additional income would more than justify the cost of having a cleaner and an immaculate house would give a much better impression to my customers – perhaps I could even start adding to the rainy-day pot that had never reached a significant amount before it was raided and depleted again.

I found Jean tactful and unobtrusive, and we soon got into a habit of sharing a sandwich at midday, often whether she was working or not.

'I have the feeling you skip meals when you're busy,' she said, eyeing me critically. 'There's nothing of you and, if you don't mind me saying so, you look a bit peaky at times.'

It was only when she said it that I realized Jean was right. I had been feeling a bit off-colour, though it was nothing I could really put my finger on, a general lethargy that really got in the way of my resolve to make better use of my time. From working around the clock with no ill effects, I suddenly found I sometimes had a job to climb the stairs to my sewing room and, for someone who had always had boundless energy, that was quite disconcerting.

However, an unexpected phone call from Megan lifted my spirits and my energy levels.

'Can't stop,' she said. 'They're cramming a lot in to these weeks before we start community, but while we still have weekends off I'm going to nip home. I'll be there late Friday for one night or maybe two. Oh, and I've told Dad we'll all go out for a meal together, while I'm down, because you two are getting on so well and time will be short. That's all right, isn't it?'

CHAPTER TWELVE

I stood there with the phone pressed to my ear and my mouth opening and shutting, though no words were coming out. Sitting down for a meal with Chay was the very last thing I wanted to do, but what could I say?

'Of course it is, Meggie.' The words sounded forced, even to my ears, so I tried harder, made my tone light, bright and enthusiastic. 'Of *course* it is. I'll look forward to it and especially to seeing you.'

It wasn't her fault. It was only natural that our daughter should want to spend what limited time she had at home with both her parents. Megan had no idea what had happened between us or about the resulting uneasiness – on my part more so than there appeared to be on Chay's, it had to be admitted.

Of course, and very typically, Martin's rearranged plans for the cancelled weekend clashed with Megan arriving home and, though he tried very hard to be understanding, to say he was miffed was a huge understatement. I had to get quite cross with him.

'I can understand that you're disappointed,' I told him, adding firmly, 'but this is my daughter we're talking about, my only child, and once the course gets going, the times I will get to see her will be extremely limited. This weekend is a huge and unexpected bonus for me.'

'But I've booked and arranged everything,' he protested. 'Made sure that everything will be extra special to make up for last week.'

'It would have been sensible to have checked with me first,' I pointed out as gently as I could. 'You will just have to change the booking, I'm afraid,' I paused, and then went on, 'Or take someone else.'

I heard the sudden intake of breath, right down the phone, and realizing that I had probably finally blown any chance of a meaningful relationship between us, I did take a minute to wonder what the hell I was playing at. Martin wasn't the kind of man you could throw ultimatums at and get away with it.

'I might just do that,' he said huffily.

'That's entirely up to you,' I said, without the hint of a tremor in my tone, I was pleased to note. 'Goodbye, Martin,' I added abruptly.

'I didn't mean that,' he said quickly and I let out the breath I was holding. 'Don't put the phone down. I'm in Brussels next weekend, but I'll sort something out. What about the weekend after that?'

'I'll keep it clear,' I promised, then found myself agreeing to an evening out after Megan had gone back and before he left for Brussels.

I put the phone down and stared at it, knowing I had surprised Martin and also surprised myself. I was suddenly realizing what was meant by the saying, *treat 'em mean and keep 'em keen*. It seemed that the majority of men didn't appreciate a doormat, after all. What a pity it had taken so long for me to realize that.

Megan arrived in a flurry of activity, dumping her bulging holdall next to the washing machine, just as she always had after any time away from home. Then she checked the oven and, laughing, rushed to give me a huge hug.

'I knew it, shepherd's pie. I told the girls you would have my favourite meal waiting and they were so envious.'

'It's their favourite, too?'

'No, but most of them don't have a mum like you, by the sounds of it. Can I have a bath? I can't wait to have a soak with candles lit and some of your best bath oil.'

'I'll turn the oven down,' I promised, already loading the washing machine from the bag next to it. 'Take as long as you like.'

I hadn't been expecting Chay and yet, when I opened the door to him, I wasn't surprised at all. It was obvious he would be as desperate to see Megan as I was, despite the relatively short time she'd been gone.

'Is it OK for me to come round?' he asked, quite humbly and for all the world as if he hadn't been turning up at every opportunity, uninvited, just recently.

I opened the door wider and forced a smile. 'Yes, it's fine, come in.'

He'd brought flowers and some of Megan's favourite chocolates.

Thrusting the pretty bouquet into my hands he said, 'These are for you.'

As I cut stems and put the flowers into a vase I mused that the house was beginning to look and smell like a florist's shop. With flowers already in the hall and sitting room I placed these on the kitchen windowsill and had to admit they did brighten up the room and lend a subtle fragrance to the aroma of the shepherd's pie.

He looked round. 'Where's Megan? Her car's outside.'

I nodded, managed a rueful smile and pointed to the washing machine and then the oven. 'Laundry and shepherd's pie are also clues pointing to her presence, as is the music playing upstairs. She's having a bath.' I handed him a chilled bottle of Chardonnay and the corkscrew. 'Perhaps you'll do the honours. You'll stay and eat with us, of course?'

He seemed to hesitate.

'Silly of me.' I jumped in before he could refuse. 'You'll have other plans. That's fine, no worries.'

'No.' The cork slid out easily with an audible plop and he concentrated on pouring the pale liquid into one of the waiting glasses, only meeting my gaze with a straight one of his own as he handed it to me. 'I would love to stay. Just wasn't sure how welcome I would be.'

'Meggie is your daughter too. It's only natural you want

131

to spent some of the short time she's here with her and I don't begrudge you that. I'm sure we can manage to be civil for a few hours.'

'Of course. Thank you for your understanding,' he said formally.

We didn't have to try very hard to get along, since Megan did most of the talking once she came downstairs wrapped in her favourite scruffy bathrobe and with her old furry boot slippers on her feet.

'It's so-o-o lovely to be home,' she sighed, digging into her second big helping of pie and vegetables, 'and enjoying its comforts.' She smiled happily at us both. 'Not that I'm not enjoying every moment of the course, though it's barely started and there is so-o-o much to remember. But this is lovely, and I have missed you both – and Tom, a lot.'

Megan didn't sound regretful or sad, which was a relief, and from then on the conversation centred on what she had been doing, what she had learned, the friends she had made, where she lived, and university life in general from a student midwife's point of view. All Chay and I had to do was to offer a comment or a question at appropriate moments and so the evening passed very pleasantly. Eventually, I think we both relaxed a bit and were able to enjoy our daughter's company and even each other's to an extent.

Exhausted from the drive, the excitement of coming home and relaxed from the half-glass of wine she had consumed, Megan eventually fell asleep on the couch, while I was clearing the remains of the meal away. Chay called me and we stood in the doorway together, looking at her.

'We can't leave her there. I'd better wake her,' I said, taking a step into the room.

'No,' he put a hand on my arm, 'don't disturb her. I'll carry her upstairs.'

I couldn't help smiling as I reminded him, 'She's eighteen now, Chay, not eight.'

'I can manage,' he insisted, and he did. In fact he was barely out of breath as he settled her into bed and I covered her with the duvet I had pulled back in readiness.

'She's changed already,' Chay said as we stood side by side enjoying the sight of our daughter in her own home and tucked into her own bed. 'She's growing up.'

'Yes,' I nodded and reached down to smooth back a strand of hair from her face. 'She is.'

I straightened and turned away, blinking a silly tear from my eye. Chay had also turned to go and there was an embarrassing moment when we both tried to fit through the doorway at the same time.

'Are you crying?' He'd let me through first but caught up with me on the landing.

'No,' I denied, shaking my head emphatically and blinking any lingering moisture away.

'You've done a great job with Megan.'

'So have you.'

'Thank you,' we said in unison, and then laughed a

little nervously.

The tension that had been missing while we had Megan's company was back, as was the pull of attraction; I was forced to accept that, even though I didn't understand it. I hurried to put a distance between us, stumbled at the top of the stairs and would have fallen if Chay hadn't grabbed me and in one swift movement pulled me round and into his arms.

'I have you,' he said, and there was a sudden stillness between us.

I licked lips that were suddenly dry and his gaze followed the tiny movement, his brown eyes darkened, and although I wasn't aware that either of us had moved, our mouths were suddenly so close that I could smell Chay's aftershave and feel his breath on my face.

A sudden small sound from Megan's room had us leaping apart like scalded cats. I rushed to my daughter's side, only to find her still as soundly asleep as when we had left her – was it really only moments ago?

We were scarcely able to meet each other's gaze and Chay left soon afterwards. I closed the door firmly behind him and took myself off to bed, determined not to give what had almost happened between us any importance by dwelling on it at all.

Easier said than done, I found when, waking in the early hours, I couldn't get out of my head the disturbing thought that I wasn't sure whether to be pleased or sorry that, in the end, nothing had actually happened between us at all.

*

I was pegging out the washing on what was a brisk autumn Saturday morning, when Megan put her tousled head around the kitchen door, and between chews on a piece of toast, said, 'Well, I have to say I'm impressed. You *have* been busy since I've been gone.'

Thinking she'd taken a peek into the sewing room at the amount of completed orders hanging ready for collection on the rails dotted around the room, I was about to comment that my orders were pretty much up to date, when she disabused me of the notion that her comment was work related.

'The house looks *lovely*, even the windows are sparkling. I'm impressed, though it seems a bit late in the year for spring cleaning.'

I grinned ruefully, lifted the line with the aid of the clothes prop and said as I walked towards Megan, 'Sorry to disappoint you, but I haven't lifted a finger unless it involved dressmaking.'

Over a fresh cup of tea and more toast, I told her about my meeting with Jean. 'Such a nice lady,' I enthused. 'We've become real friends. I can't think what took us so long.'

'You scarcely went out of the house,' Megan reminded me, barely looking up from the business of spreading butter, very thickly, on to another piece of toast. 'Unless,' she added, around an impressive mouthful, 'I forced you out shopping. Is she married?'

135

'Widowed. Late husband was a bit of a misery and she makes no secret of it, so she probably didn't get out much either.' I looked around a kitchen that was spotless, apart from the crumbs around the toaster and around my daughter's plate and her mouth. 'She's made a difference to my life in more ways than one. You must meet her.'

'Who's that?' asked Chay nosily, walking unannounced through the back door. 'Your side gate was unlocked,' he added by way of explanation, 'so I thought I'd save you the bother of answering the front door. I could tell you were up by the washing on the line. Is there any of that toast left? I'm starving.'

Millicent obviously wasn't one for breakfast, was my first thought, but I swiftly dismissed it as none of my business and, indicating the toaster and bread bin, advised, 'Help yourself. I was talking about Jean, the lady with the dog you saw the other day.'

I could have bitten off my tongue when I noticed Megan's sudden interest and I guessed I'd made it sound as if Chay was round at my house all the time. Well, perhaps he was, I corrected myself, but not at my invitation, and I didn't want Megan getting ideas about a parents' reunion again.

'It was the day Martin was here, remember?' I added, even though I knew Chay wouldn't want reminding.

'Oh, yes, Martin.' I could almost see the eagerness seep out of Megan, and she put the piece of toast she had been devouring back on her plate as if her appetite was quite gone. 'How is he? I suppose all the flowers are down to him, are they?'

'By way of an apology for letting me down over last weekend, though he has already rearranged it, and I'm meeting him for a meal in the week before he leaves for Brussels.'

'Great,' Megan said, with a distinct lack of enthusiasm, and she took herself off to get ready soon after. I did the same, leaving Chay to read the weekend papers.

He rose gallantly to tell us we both looked gorgeous when we came back down, 'More like sisters,' he added, which I thought was over-egging the pudding a bit.

'I doubt Megan will be too pleased at having you say she looks a similar age to her mother, Cha-rlie.'

'Actually, I don't mind at all, Mum, because you do look great for your age – and I love that jacket. Where did you get it?'

I looked down at the bouclé material in a blue-grey mix that I had made into a little fitted short coat that did look well with my jeans, I thought. 'Why, I made it, and I'm in the middle of making one for Jean. In a different colour, of course.'

'I'd love it if you would make me one next.' Megan was eyeing the jacket as if it carried a designer label. 'I absolutely love it.'

'It's as good as done,' I assured her.

'I suppose a new suit for me is out of the question?' Chay queried, and we all laughed as we left the house and piled into the four by four he had parked at the kerb.

Being early, we had our pick of the local pubs and were

soon settled around a table with the offerings of a delicious carvery piled on the plates in front of us. The atmosphere was easy, the conversation flowed, and it was all most enjoyable. I doubted an outsider would have been able to tell that there was a fracture, a hairline crack, through this seemingly happy family unit.

However, visible or not, it was there, and I was going to have to be the one to make sure it was a permanent break. It had been too easy to excuse my lack of progress in tracking down the elusive decree absolute on everything that had happened lately – but I was going to have to make it a priority for all of our sakes. It would be the proof, if proof was needed, that there was absolutely no going back for Chay and me.

CHAPTER THIRTEEN

'I thought I would go and see Gran this afternoon and maybe Tom's parents as well, or a couple of friends,' Megan said, after she had practically licked the last of the treacle pudding and custard from her bowl. 'You don't mind, do you?'

'No, of course not,' Chay and I said immediately and together. 'Shall we come with you?'

'No, you don't have to do that, you can see Gran any time,' she said. 'I thought somebody mentioned a walk on the beach, so why don't you carry on and do that? I'll be home later to share a meal with you both, and then I intend to have an early night and leave after breakfast in the morning. I can make my own way to Gran's from here and everyone else is within walking distance, so I'll leave you to it and see you both later at Mum's.'

She was gone before either of us could say a word and we sat in stunned silence for a moment.

I tried to make light of it by saying, 'Sorry, it looks as if you're stuck with me again – unless you have other plans?'

Chay shook his head, and apologized, 'And you've been volunteered to feed me, yet again.'

'It's no trouble – really.' I didn't sound convincing even to my own ears.

'Perhaps a walk along the beach is a good idea,' he said, adding a bit awkwardly, 'We should talk, clear the air.'

I didn't feel I had much choice but to agree but, as soon as I'd climbed into his car I was wishing myself elsewhere and wondered why I hadn't just asked him to drop me at home. The answer was, obviously, that he would have very likely joined me there, so perhaps the beach was a better option, after all.

Nothing much was said on the journey, apart from comments on the traffic and the weather. There was a surprising number of cars in the car park and we agreed that we hadn't expected that, now the warm weather was just about over.

'Dog-walkers, of course,' I said, as we came within sight of the sea and sand.

'Almost makes you wish you had one,' Chay commented. 'A couple of my lads bring their dogs to work sometimes, and they sit in their owner's vehicles as patient as you like, knowing they'll get a run in the breaks and a few titbits.'

'Jean was trying to persuade me to get one the other day, but it doesn't seem fair, even though I'm at home all day. I don't think dogs – or cats – and dressmaking would sit well together. You know, delicate materials with all that fur, not to mention muddy pawprints.'

'Not a good combination,' Chay agreed.

'And I often work without a break for hours. A dog needs regular walks.'

'Do I get the impression that you quite like the idea but you're trying to put yourself off?'

'Mmmm.' I tried to be non-committal.

'Might be good for you to have a reason to take regular breaks, and the fresh air would certainly do you good. It can't be great for your health to be cooped up indoors for hours at a time.'

I threw a ball for a bouncy black Labrador who had dropped it right at my feet, laughing when he brought it straight back to me in no time at all. 'Pets are very tying and time consuming. What if I wanted to go away?'

I was thinking about Martin and the weekend, but knew I might also want to take myself on a real holiday at some point. It had been cheap and cheerful caravan breaks while Megan was growing up and nowhere further than the Isle of Wight, but it might be a good time to treat myself, with work starting to pick up.

'There's always your mum, or I could help,' Chay added, surprising me.

'You?' I stared at him.

'There's no reason we can't be friends, is there?' He shrugged, and pulled his mouth into a straight line. 'You've made it clear there will be nothing more and I accept that now. What happened between us was a one off; you were upset about Megan leaving home, I tried to comfort you, and it got a bit out of hand. Nothing more to it than that.'

Chay saw my look and put his hands up. 'OK, OK, I won't mention it again. I just wanted you to know that I realize, in spite of the fact we're probably still married, that there is no chance of a repeat performance, much less a reconciliation. I can settle for being friends if you can.'

'That would be good, if only for Megan's sake,' I agreed.

It was only later as we were on our way home that I took the time to digest fully what he had said and to wonder what exactly – if anything – it was that he *had* been hoping for.

No chance of a repeat performance, much less a reconciliation. What on earth did that mean? The idea of a repeat performance, I could understand might have a certain appeal. We had always been very compatible in bed, and still were going by recent experience. The memory still made me blush to my ears, but reconciliation? After all these years? The very idea was laughable.

And what about Millicent? Where did she fit in to all of this? Millicent pushing Chay to set the date for their marriage had started this whole business and now she was conspicuous by her absence, even as a topic of conversation. I glanced at Chay out of the corner of my eye and successfully fought the urge to show any interest, reminding myself that their relationship was absolutely

142

none of my business. Anyway, I didn't want to give the impression that I cared about them or their up-coming marriage, because, of course, I didn't.

I refused to eat shepherd's pie for two days running, even for Megan, but I had frozen the extra one I'd made the day before for her to take back with her. Today we were having tuna pasta bake, which was another of her favourites, and I went to work with the ingredients, advising Chay to set the table and open the bottle of wine that had been cooling in the fridge.

'This is so nice,' Megan said with her mouth full. 'Well worth coming home for. Not just the food, which is fabulous by the way, but seeing you two getting along so well.'

'We should have thought of it from your point of view years ago,' I said regretfully. 'Made a much bigger effort to get along and behave like adults instead of squabbling kids after we separated.'

'So what went wrong?' she asked. 'Why did you separate, if you don't mind me asking? And why was there so much animosity between you? You must have been in love once, so what happened to change that? I've always wondered but the topic was kind of taboo.'

'Married much too young,' Chay said bluntly. 'Simple as that.'

'Well, that together with not enough money coming in and too much going out for us to keep to a budget,' I said with feeling. 'We were always overdrawn. They say when debt comes in the door, love flies out of the window, and

143

that just about sums it up for us. Wouldn't you agree, Charlie?'

It wasn't said in an accusing tone, but Chay looked as if he wanted to argue some point. However, Megan spoke before he did.

'You obviously didn't have to get married, since I wasn't born until well after your wedding. You've always insisted that I wasn't an accident, yet you had a child – me – when you must have already been struggling. Why?'

Why, indeed? What could we say? That it had seemed like a good idea at the time? In truth we should have waited, but our baby had been a vain and desperate attempt to hold a very shaky marriage together. In reality, having Megan, the one good thing to come out of our relationship, had, in fact, been the final straw. The enormous additional burden on already strained finances meant that we literally couldn't find a way to survive together. In the end, love just hadn't been enough.

To my relief Chay spoke up, and I was very interested to hear his take on what had happened. If for no other reason than that I wanted to see if it matched my own.

'We loved each other and we loved and wanted you,' he assured Megan, 'but lack of money and common sense is a killer when it comes to relationships. We just rushed into everything too soon. We were too young for all the responsibility and should have had the sense to take things slowly and get our professional lives established first. By rushing into marriage at a young age – your age – we threw away the chance of the careers we had planned and the financial security they could have given us.'

'You shouldn't have had me.'

'You,' I insisted, 'are the one thing – perhaps the only thing – we got right.'

'Absolutely.' Chay placed great emphasis on that one word.

'You lived with Gran and Grandad after you split up, didn't you?' Megan obviously wasn't going to let the matter drop. 'Why didn't Dad come, too?'

Why indeed? I thought but stayed silent, leaving it to Chay to explain – if he could.

He mumbled a bit, then he said, with a shamed look on his face, and what appeared to be total honesty, 'My pride wouldn't let me. What would that look like? A man who couldn't support his own family expecting his in-laws, who were more than willing to take in their daughter and granddaughter, to provide a home for him, too?'

'They wouldn't have minded and I know they understood that you had tried your best. You weren't much more than a boy,' I protested, trying at last to see things from his point of view. I had never really done that before, if I was honest.

'Old enough to marry and start a family. I had to prove to myself, to them and to you, too, that I was man enough to provide for them. There was precious little in the way of decent jobs on offer locally, so I had to widen the net in order to start earning a reasonable wage.'

But he hadn't had to go to the other side of the world to

do that and he'd had no need to forget that he had a wife at home in England. With those thoughts I hardened my heart. A heart that was beginning to soften alarmingly towards the man whose behaviour at that difficult time had resulted in the ending of our young and, to me at least, precious marriage. I felt he had abandoned both Megan and me; had turned his back on us both to start a single life elsewhere. No amount of money could make up for that.

'It seems a shame,' Megan commented.

'It will be different for you and Tom if – when – you decide to settle down. You have far more sense than to make the mistakes that we made and life will be so much easier as a result. I envy you,' I added, and I really did.

How could I help wondering how different things would have been for Chay and me if only we had waited, been as sensible as Megan and Tom. A glance at his expression told me he was having similar and completely pointless thoughts of his own.

'Together or apart, you're still the best parents I could have wished for,' Megan said firmly, and getting up, she yawned, kissed us both goodnight and said over her shoulder, 'I'll see you both in the morning.'

Chay shook his head as the door closed behind her. 'Were we ever that sensible?'

'I really don't think so and I don't know what exactly we did to deserve a daughter like Megan.'

'Nor me either,' he said, and started helping me to clear the table before I remembered the washing still out on the line and left him to it.

He seemed in no hurry to leave, taking his time to stack the dishwasher, and then making coffee for us both, so I set to and tackled the ironing. After all, it wasn't late and it would save me a job in the morning.

I began to think he would never go, even wondered if he was waiting for me to invite him to stay the night. It was something I had no intention of doing, mainly because it would give Megan completely the wrong idea – and Chay, too, probably.

I closed the door behind him at last with a huge sigh of relief and admitted to myself that I was finding it quite unsettling having him around so much after years of barely setting eyes on him, though I wasn't quite sure why.

It seemed no time at all until I was opening the door to let him in again, freshly shaved and showered, and looking just a bit too attractive for my peace of mind.

'I thought we could go out to breakfast,' he said, almost bouncing into the hall.

'Nice idea,' I said, a trifle tartly, 'but the offer comes a bit late because – as you can probably tell – the bacon is already sizzling under the grill.'

In truth, going out would have been a great idea because the smell was making me feel quite queasy. I wondered if the vague symptoms I had experienced when I was with Jean were still hanging around, but it was probably just the fact that I'd never been one for cooked breakfasts anyway, much preferring toast or cereal to start the day.

It was obvious that neither Megan or Chay had such reservations as they tucked in with gusto. Egg, bacon, sausage, beans, tomatoes and fried bread were helped down by several slices of buttered toast until I began to wonder where they were putting it all. Both were oblivious to the fact that I was merely pushing my rapidly cooling food around an unappetisingly greasy plate, willing them to hurry up so that I could clear it all away.

Chay checked Megan's car for oil and water. The extra shepherds pie I had made was joined by an apple crumble, a home-made fruitcake, and a packed lunch for the journey.

'It's been lovely.' She threw her arms first around my neck and then around Chay's, and we stood together at the kerbside long after she had driven out of sight.

It was only when we eventually made a move to go indoors that I realized he had been standing all that time with his arm around my shoulders and, what was more, I was shocked to discover that I really didn't mind.

CHAPTER FOURTEEN

The feeling lasted right up until I glanced over my shoulder and realized that Martin had pulled up in his sports car and was sitting at the wheel looking at the pair of us linked together with a quizzical expression on his good-looking face.

I shrugged off Chay's arm as if it was suddenly burning me right through my clothes and hurried over to his car.

'Martin, what a lovely surprise. What are you doing here?'

'I kind of guessed Megan would make an early start, and thought lunch might take your mind off her leaving – but if you're busy. . . .' he indicated Chay standing in the middle of the path. He was looking so disgruntled that I wondered whether he might have had plans of his own for the two of us – and exactly what they might have been.

No, the idea that he was still lusting after me was ridiculous. He had a life of his own – and a lady of his own – to get back to.

'Not busy at all,' I said airily and loudly enough for Chay to hear. 'Charlie has to get back to the lovely Millicent and,' I added with truth, remembering the barely touched breakfast, 'I'm starving. Just give me a minute and I'll be with you.'

I swept past the frowning Chay, and rushed inside to run a brush through my hair, and gather my jacket and handbag. I was applying fresh lipstick when Chay appeared in the doorway.

'What do you think you're doing?'

'What does it look like?' I held out my hands and then made a circle in front of my face with one of them to indicate my appearance. 'Getting ready to go out to lunch with Martin.'

'And what about us?'

'You know as well as I do, Charlie, there is no *us*. Go home to Millicent and make your wedding plans, because I will definitely make time during this coming week to do what needs to be done to finalize our divorce.' I pushed past him. 'Make sure you slam the door on your way out.'

As soon as I was safely in the car, Martin roared off and I successfully fought the urge to glance back.

'Where would you like to go?' Martin asked, and I was pleased that he also successfully fought a very natural urge to ask what the hell was going on with Chay and me, because I could completely understand what the touching little display of togetherness back there on the pavement might have looked like.

In the months I'd known Martin he couldn't have failed to be aware of the animosity I had always felt towards Chay. I had rarely mentioned my ex-husband's name, but when I did it had practically been snarled, and now suddenly it must seem that he was forever on my doorstep and getting closer by the minute. It would be unusual if the recent change in our relationship hadn't invited comment, yet he wisely held his tongue, which I did appreciate.

'Just somewhere casual would probably be best.' I indicated my jean-clad legs and suede jacket.

'A country pub?' Martin suggested and I responded, 'Lovely,' settling back in the seat, determined to leave explanations – should they be called for until later.

The CD playing softly was music from the eighties, which I knew wasn't Martin's taste at all. I couldn't fail to be touched, realizing that he had chosen it to please me. There was no doubt his attitude towards me had changed in recent weeks. It was far from the casual, almost cavalier and very off-hand approach I was used to from him and I did wonder what had brought it about and where it was leading.

As if to emphasize the change Martin said suddenly, 'Thank you for coming out with me at such short notice.'

Shocked, I knew I would have fallen out of my seat had I not been in the confines of a car and belted in. 'Thank you for thinking of me,' I said. 'Megan coming home again so soon, lovely as it was to see her, was quite unsettling. I had only just begun to get used to her not

151

being there.'

'Is it a good thing – you and Charlie getting on so well these days?'

There it was: the question I had been expecting, but very nicely put. There was no accusation in Martin's tone that I could detect, only polite interest. If he was bothered about Charlie being around so much, he was being very careful not to show it.

'Well, yes, it is,' I turned a little in my seat, so that I could face him, 'for Megan. The two of us being at loggerheads for so many years can't have been good for her as a child, and I know we both regret it now.'

Parking in front of a pretty little thatched pub far enough from Brankstone to make you feel you were in the wilds of the beautifully autumnal Dorset countryside brought the conversation to a natural end.

Martin was round to open my door and help me out with a speed that impressed me, and he kept my hand tucked into his own as we entered the long low building and were quickly shown to a table.

We both ordered sparkling water, Martin because he was driving and me because I thought alcohol might upset a stomach that, thankfully, appeared to have settled down since breakfast time.

The crab mousse starter was delicious and Martin appeared to enjoy his duck pâté. We were making inroads into roast beef and all the trimmings when Martin dropped his bombshell.

'He's still in love with you, you know.'

I was taking a sip of water at the time and choked as it went down the wrong way. I coughed, took another sip and coughed some more, and with eyes streaming demanded, 'What? Who?'

'Charlie. It's very obvious that he wants you back. I'm surprised he hasn't said as much; he doesn't seem the type to let the grass grow under his feet.'

'He's let the grass grow under his feet, as you put it, for more years than I care to mention. No, Martin, you couldn't be more wrong, I assure you.'

I picked up my knife and fork dismissively, cut into beef that was quite rare in the middle and felt my traitorous stomach rebel at the sight of the pink meat. The next minute I was running towards the toilet with my serviette pressed to my lips. Very grateful for the clarity of the signage, I made it just in time and emerged, white and shaking, a good few minutes later.

'Are you OK? You look terrible.'

Martin's concern seemed very genuine, as did that of the waitress, and I hastened to assure them both that I was fine. I didn't want them to imagine I had food poisoning and neither did I mention the recurring nausea to either of them in case they might think it was something catching. I did think I should have stayed at home for more reasons than one.

'Nothing to do with the food.' I did my best to be reassuring while averting my eyes from the half-eaten food now congealing on the plate. Luckily, Martin had as good as finished.

'What about a brandy to settle your stomach?' he suggested.

I agreed gratefully. The waitress rushed off, returning within seconds to place a glass in front of me and the smooth liquid burning its way down through my body did seem to do the trick almost immediately. I could actually feel the colour returning to my cheeks.

'I'm so sorry,' I said, when the waitress had gone, taking the plates with her and patently relieved to see me looking better.

'You have nothing to apologize for.'

'But I've ruined lunch for you.'

'Nonsense, I was as good as finished anyway. I'm just sorry you didn't enjoy yours.' I did feel bad about it and almost felt obliged to suggest, 'What about a pudding?' and then felt that, actually, I might manage something light myself, since I already felt so much better, and I added as much.

Martin looked really pleased, asking for the dessert menu and encouraging me to make my choice first. 'An ice cream,' he suggested helpfully. 'That should be light enough, don't you think?'

I laughed, sure that I had suffered the last of the nausea and was actually really hungry. 'Do you know, what I would really enjoy more than anything is good old Bramley apple pie and custard.'

He looked at me for a moment as if I was quite mad, then he laughed too, and said, 'Apple pie it is, then, and I'll join you. I haven't eaten that since I was a kid. Now I think about it, it used to be a favourite of mine.'

The Martin I had known, or thought I had known these last few months would never have admitted to ever having been a child, much less admit to enjoying anything as humble as an apple pie.

'You've never mentioned your childhood before,' I told him while we waited for our chosen desserts to arrive.

'It wasn't a particularly happy one.' He shrugged. 'Megan doesn't know how lucky she is having two parents who care enough about her to put her first.'

'Well, I had that, too, and they always stood by me, even when I blotted my copybook badly by rushing into a teenage marriage and destroying all the dreams they had for me and my own dreams in the process.'

'You were pregnant with Megan?' Martin guessed, making the assumption that most people made about youthful weddings.

The apple pie, accompanied by a huge jug of custard, arrived and I couldn't wait to tuck in, suddenly ravenously hungry.

Speaking with my mouth full, I said, 'No, not pregnant, just young and impetuous, without a brain cell between us. My parents were there to pick up the pieces when we split up, or else I don't know what I'd have done. By then we'd lost everything, including our home. Megan and I went to live with my parents and Charlie went abroad to find work. He said it was where the money was.'

Martin paused with a spoonful of pie halfway to his mouth. 'You sound bitter.'

'He could have found work in England if he'd wanted. It seemed to me that he gave up on us. Well, me, anyway,' I admitted honestly, 'because he always kept in touch with Megan. He was and is a very good dad.'

'I used to think I would be – one day – but here I am all grown up and no closer to having a family. I think the childhood I had made me over cautious about close relationships and probably extremely self-centred. Things change, though, and I think I would be able to settle for a stable relationship with the right person now. I never thought I would hear myself say that.'

He was looking at me in a way that left me in little doubt that the 'right person' he was thinking of settling down with was probably me. I just knew I wasn't ready for the declaration that might be about to follow.

I totally flipped, leaping to my feet, snatching my jacket from the back of the chair and saying, 'I really think I need to get some air. Do you mind if we leave now?'

If Martin had been about to get down on one knee – which was an unlikely and ludicrous idea – or even broach the old-fashioned suggestion that we 'went steady', he hid it well and was all concern again. After helping me into my jacket he quickly paid the bill, and had me settled into the car in no time.

In truth, the queasiness had quite gone and I was regretting the discarded remains of the apple pie. However, I kept up the pretence by having the window down on my side and acknowledging Martin's suggestion of a visit to my GP as sensible.

'Probably a twenty-four-hour thing.' I tried to sound dismissive and carefully ignored the symptoms I'd suffered a few days previously. 'More inconvenient than anything else. I can't afford to be ill right now because I have a busy day with customers tomorrow.'

'I was going to suggest a walk, but it'll probably be best if you go home to bed. Do you have any milk of magnesia in the cupboard? If not I could stop off and get some on the way. It might help. In fact,' he added with a close look at me,' it might be a good idea for me to come home with you. It's not a good idea to be alone when you're feeling so poorly, you know.'

He took some persuading but I eventually convinced him that I would be better off alone. This sensitive, caring side of Martin was very new and I wasn't sure it would survive living with the physical reality of a stomach bug. I might have my reservations about us working out as a long-term couple but I didn't want to destroy any apparent illusions he might have in that direction just yet.

Martin had taken some persuading not to come inside to see me tucked up safely in bed, and more assurances were needed that I would indeed seek medical help first thing in the morning, before he finally drove away.

I turned the key in the front door wearily, wondering what on earth was happening in my life. I was sensible enough to know that nothing stays the same and I had expected to experience the empty nest syndrome when

Megan left. What I hadn't been expecting was to have Chay re-entering my life or the confused feelings I would experience about that, or the complication of my casual relationship with Martin – if you could have even called what we had a relationship – changing into something else that I clearly wasn't ready for practically overnight.

I was so deep in thought as I hung my coat on the peg that I almost keeled over with shock when I turned round to find Chay standing behind me in the sitting room doorway.

'Jesus, Chay,' I blasted furiously, 'you almost gave me a heart attack. What the hell are you still doing here?'

'Well, I started tidying up a bit. You went off in such a rush that the breakfast things were left and Megan's things strewn everywhere. I didn't think you'd want to come back to that. I've just about finished. I wasn't expecting you back so soon.'

'Very kind of you, I'm sure,' I said sarcastically. I was actually quite glad not to have to face the mess but wouldn't have admitted that to Chay, not in a million years. 'Don't you have something better to be getting on with, with your *girlfriend*?'

'Maybe later,' he muttered, and I wondered if they'd had a row or something. 'Sorry, I didn't mean to get under your feet. As I already said, I wasn't expecting you back so soon. Actually, are you all right? You look a bit peaky.'

'Bit of a tummy bug,' I dismissed. 'It's nothing.'

Chay nodded and reached for his coat. 'Probably something going around. Not like you to be ill, though.

Always had the constitution of an ox, as I remember –
except when you were. . . .'

We stared at each other, similar horrified realization in
the eyes of both of us.

'Pregnant,' he finished, and watched helplessly as I
burst into tears.

CHAPTER FIFTEEN

For the second time that day I ran to the toilet, but this time my nausea had less to do with any stomach upset, and everything to do with a situation that made everything else that had happened in my life recently fade into insignificance.

I crept into the kitchen and found Chay waiting with what I assumed was a cup of the hot, sweet tea that he must have been told somewhere along the way was good for shock. I noticed he had also made himself one – and rather more than a hint of hysterical laughter began to bubble up inside me. It was immediately suppressed. I didn't need reminding that this was no laughing matter.

I sank down on to a chair before my legs gave out on me. 'What am I going to do?' I implored. 'What the hell am I going to do?'

'What are *we* going to do?' Chay corrected, 'This is my problem, too.'

I took a sip of tea and then pushed the cup away. I

didn't need reminding that tea wasn't going to help. 'Why don't you just take off?' I glared at him. 'It's what you did before.'

'I was a boy then,' he protested, 'as you so rightly pointed out only recently. You're not the girl you were back then, either, and I doubt very much that you'll be running home to your mother this time.'

' "Running. . . ." How dare you, Chay. I had no choice. I had a child to think of and no other home to go to.' I was on my feet by this time, my hands pressed flat to the table between us, practically screaming into Chay's face. 'Would you have preferred to see Megan and myself on the streets?'

'Sorry, sorry. That came out all wrong.'

'This mess is all wrong. Why the hell couldn't you have stayed out of my life, Chay? Wasn't messing it up the once enough for you?'

I could have bitten off my tongue even as the words left my mouth, even while I was acknowledging that there was a certain truth to them. There was an almighty crash as the front door slammed so hard behind Chay's undoubtedly furious back that I could swear I felt the walls shake. Then there was complete silence, until the telephone started to ring. I wouldn't have had the energy to get up and answer it even if I had felt inclined – which I definitely did not.

The answer phone clicked in and I heard Martin's deep voice. It was the same voice that had sent shivers down my spine only a relatively short time ago, back in the days when I'd considered myself extremely lucky to be allotted an hour or two of his time when he could spare it. If I was being truthful I still wasn't quite sure what someone like him could possibly see in someone like me. 'I hope I didn't wake you, darling? I was just very concerned about you today and hope you're feeling better.'

'Oh, absolutely, Martin,' I said aloud and with deep irony, 'never felt better in my life,' and wondered when exactly things had changed between us. Why, when he had suddenly become more interested in me as a person, had I become less enamoured of him?

'If you feel up to it, you have my number,' Martin continued, but I realized that in fact I didn't have his number. I had never had Martin's number because it had always been he who rang me when it was convenient to him. It was just one thing that had always made me insecure about our relationship; there were many others, though I couldn't be bothered to dwell on what those were right now. 'Call me any time,' he was urging, 'and as soon as you feel better we can start making up for lost time.'

I managed a wry smile in the direction of the phone, and wondered how keen he was going to be 'to make up for lost time' when he knew exactly what had caused me to be under the weather. Then I forgot all about him and went back to wondering what I was going to do about the unbelievable situation I found myself in.

I still couldn't believe I had been such an idiot. Falling into bed with an ex-husband was a grave error of judgement, but to do so without a single thought of the consequences had been a mistake of epic proportions that was going to cost me dearly in more ways than one. Wishing with all my heart that I could turn back time was a totally futile exercise, but I found myself doing it anyway.

A baby at my time of life was a difficult enough proposition. A baby resulting from a thoughtless fling at my time of life was absolutely unthinkable. What would people think? The neighbours? I realized without humour that I was in danger of sounding like my mother.

Oh, God, I heard myself gasp out loud. My *mother*. What on earth was she going to say? And then I put my head into my hands and groaned. Never mind my mother, what the hell was my *daughter* going to say? I ran to the toilet again and then returned to sit wretchedly at the table to contemplate a future that was looking bleaker by the minute.

How embarrassing for a woman of my age to have to confess to her level-headed daughter that she was pregnant and from what amounted to nothing more than a one-night stand. What on earth was I going to do?

The limited options open to me flitted in and out of my head. I tried to give each my careful consideration, but all I really wanted was for the whole thing to go away and let me have my normal life back. In the end I did the only thing that made any immediate sense. I took myself off to bed, buried myself under the duvet, and refused to think at all.

When I woke the sun was shining on a brand-new

bright autumn day and I was amazed that, in spite of everything, I had slept through what had remained of the preceding day and the whole of the night. I was also relieved to find that I was feeling better, physically at least, and there was no sign, so far, of yesterday's nausea. My thoughts were another matter and there was no stopping those, so I didn't even bother to try.

False alarm. That was one thought – and a very welcome one – that popped into my head when I was standing under the shower, and my spirits lifted immediately. That would be it. Of course it would. I couldn't possible be pregnant at my age, the very idea was ridiculous. There could be any number of explanations for the sickness. An actual stomach bug, for instance, which seemed most likely, but the onset of menopause wasn't totally out of the question.

By the time I was dressed and ready to face the day ahead, I had calmed down to such an extent that I'd managed to convince myself that the best course of action was simply to wait and see.

I ate a dry piece of toast, forgoing the butter I usually enjoyed spreading thickly over the bread, just as a precaution, and was sipping my tea when the doorbell went. Now, who on earth could that be?

Not Chay, I sincerely hoped, because I had only just composed myself and my equilibrium could be very easily upset again with heated and completely pointless discussions about who might be to blame if I was pregnant. Not Martin, either, because too much kindness and concern might equally prove to be my undoing.

I peered round the door. 'Jean? What are you doing here?'

She looked at me, perhaps to see if I was joking, and then said, 'I work here now, remember, and it is Monday morning.'

'Really?' I opened the door wider and stood back to let her in. 'What happened to Sunday?' I knew really, because it was all coming back to me, but I dismissed it all quickly, by explaining, 'I actually spent most of it in bed with an upset tum.'

'There,' said Jean, 'I had a feeling you were coming down with something.' We'd reached the kitchen by then and she turned to look at me a bit more closely. 'You still look a bit pale.'

'Oh, I'll be *fine* now,' I dismissed, with determined emphasis on the 'fine', and ignored the hint of yesterday's panic that had resurged from nowhere.

The affairs of the day quickly took over with the arrival of Mrs Etteridge, 'Please do call me Win, dear.' To my surprise she was accompanied by her sister, the elusive Madge.

'I know she doesn't have an appointment,' Mrs Etteridge (must remember to call her Win) said, 'but I was hoping you could squeeze her in. Show her something of what you would be able to do for her.'

'Oh, but I don't thi—' Madge looked horrified and seemed to shrink down into her long beige raincoat. I wondered what tactics Mrs – Win – had had to use to persuade her to come along at all, when it was quite clearly the last place she wanted to be.

'Nonsense, dear,' Win said firmly, and Madge's mouth snapped shut.

'Why don't you take a look at some of my sample pieces while Win has her fittings?' I suggested. 'There's no pressure on you at all to order a thing, and it won't hurt to look, will it?'

'Would you like me to bring up a tray of tea in a bit?' Jean popped her head around the kitchen doorway.

'Oh, that would be lovely. Thank you,' I said, adding for the benefit of the two elderly ladies hovering in the hallway, 'This is Jean, my good friend and neighbour.' Then ushering them towards the stairs, I encouraged, 'Shall we go on up?'

'I think I've put on a little bit since that last cruise,' Win apologized from behind the screen where she was disrobing, 'but I know you leave a bit extra on the seams, just in case.'

'No problem at all,' I soothed. 'Though I've never known you to put on as much as an ounce in all the time I've known you.'

'There, you see, Madge? You don't get that kind of service in the department stores you frequent, I'll be bound,' Win pointed out in a satisfied tone and she made department store sound like a dirty word.

I managed to ease a reluctant Madge out of her mac and guided her towards the rail of finished garments that I kept ready for customers with less set ideas or less time.

Before joining Win behind the screen I encouraged, 'Just see if there's anything you remotely like. No pressure.'

There were three outfits for Win to try, from her favoured floor-length style for evenings, to a below-the-knee floral day dress and matching bolero, and lastly a pair of white slacks, set off by a navy and white blouse. All fitted perfectly, just as I had known they would, though I fussed with the pins and tweaked the material here and there because I knew Win appreciated the extra attention.

I heard Jean come in with the tray, and the murmur of voices as she appeared to encourage Madge with a, 'What a pretty blue that is, isn't it?' and, 'A cruise – really? Oh, I would love to go on a cruise.'

When we emerged, with Win's outfits back beneath the polythene covers, to await completion, it was to find Madge holding two dresses over her arm and chatting to Jean as if she had known her all of her life.

The tea tray had been set up on a round table in the corner that was ideal for the purpose, but never used for it because I was always too busy working with the customer to offer refreshments. I was beginning to see that Jean could turn out to be a real asset.

'Do join us, Jean,' I urged.

'Oh, yes,' Madge had found her voice, 'you've been so helpful and I would really value your opinion when I try these on.'

'I'll get another cup.' Jean left the room with what

167

looked suspiciously like a wink in my direction.

'Now,' I said, as I eventually parcelled up the two outfits for Madge and closed my book on the orders for two more, 'I hope you haven't felt under any kind of pressure, and are happy with the price I've given you.'

'No,' she said with a smile that was very like her sister's, despite her plainer face. 'It's been quite enjoyable and not as expensive as I was expecting.'

'What have I been saying all this time?' Win demanded, but she was smiling, too, and they were twittering like two birds as they left the house, just as my next customer arrived.

'Is it always like this?' Jean asked, when at last we had time to sit down and eat a sandwich apiece. 'I never realized you were so busy, and now I have my doubts about those things I wanted to order. I must pay you for them at least.'

'Don't even think about it,' I told her sternly. 'You've been worth your weight in gold just this one morning.'

'Really?' She looked delighted.

'Really. I've probably ended up with double the orders because of your input. The customers love you and obviously trust your judgement. I always kept it all fairly simple with Megan growing up, but I think I could even think of expanding if you were involved, Jean, I really do. Perhaps that's something we can think about discussing if you think you might be interested.' The doorbell rang then, heralding the arrival of the first customer of the afternoon. 'When we get time, of course.' I laughed.

The rest of the day flew by. At the end of it my order book was bulging and, best of all I'd had no time at all to think. Finding that Jean had cooked the reminder of the eggs and bacon from breakfast the day before was the icing on the cake for me, because I'd have settled for a packet of Cup of Soup if left to my own devices.

'I feel like offering you a partnership right here and now,' I told her honestly, picking up my knife and fork and tucking right in.

'Now, don't get carried away.' She chuckled. 'We've only worked together for five minutes.'

'Yes, I know,' I agreed, 'but having you with me is already making a massive difference. It's very hard doing everything alone,' I added.

Jean nodded, pouring more tea for us both, 'I do understand that feeling,' she said, 'because I've spent years alone. That might sound strange knowing, as you obviously do, that I was married, but it wasn't what you could call a partnership and I certainly never felt appreciated or even very useful. I wish I'd learned a skill like you. It must be amazing to be able to support yourself.'

'The sewing is a doddle,' I went on. 'It's something I've always loved to do. I really enjoy that part of the business. I can get a lot done when I put my mind to it, and now I have you to help out around the house and with the customers I'll be able to do even more. Unfortunately, there's the paperwork too, you know, the accounts and so on. I do find that tedious, and I hate computers with a vengeance.'

Jean grimaced. 'Me, too, or I'd have been glad to help because I'm quite good with figures.' She stood up, saying, 'I must get home and walk Ben. He'll wonder what's happened to me, though I did walk him before I came here this morning and popped back after lunch as well.'

'Bring him with you tomorrow,' I said impulsively. 'I'm sure he'll be no trouble. We'll have to sort out proper hours and allow you to decide just how involved you want to be as soon as we get a quiet day. It's not fair for me to take over your life entirely and make assumptions about your time that you might not be happy with.'

The phone went then. Jean mouthed, 'We'll talk tomorrow. See you then bright and early,' and let herself out of the front door.

'Oh, hello, Mum,' I said brightly, when I had established the caller's identity. 'How are you?'

'That's what I was ringing you to ask,' she said. 'I've just had Charles on the phone and he seemed to think you had something important to tell me.'

CHAPTER SIXTEEN

What the hell was Chay thinking of, going to my mother behind my back, when I'd as good as told him this was my problem and that I would deal with it, without his help? How dare he?

'I don't appreciate the two of you discussing me behind my back.' I quickly decided that attack was my best form of defence. That, together with lying through my teeth, as in, 'And I have absolutely no idea what he's talking about.'

'He seemed *very* concerned about you, and obviously thought there was something I should know. Are you all right, Tessa?'

I was far from all right, what with the world, my ex-husband and my mother poking their noses into my affairs, but her question provided me with an answer of sorts.

'I've been a bit under the weather, but I'm feeling much better already. Charlie should have phoned me if he wanted to see how I was, instead of worrying you for no good reason.'

'But you're never ill. You rarely even get a cold. What's been wrong with you?'

'For goodness' sake, Mum, will you stop fussing?' My tone was sharp. 'I've had a bit of a bug, that's all. I am entitled to be under the weather once in a while, you know.' I thought it might have been the first time I had ever raised my voice to my mother, but I was very close to losing it with her, even though I knew she was only concerned. Bloody Chay, stirring up a hornet's nest, what on earth was he was playing at?

It seemed as if he had made his mind up I was definitely pregnant and he was getting ready to share the news with all and sundry without any discussion or a decision being made. Hadn't he ever heard of choices? If I was pregnant – and that was still in doubt – this wasn't another Megan, planned and wanted, despite our straitened circumstances at that time. This baby, if there was one, was a complete mistake and should be treated as such, not a cause for celebration.

'I'll come round,' she said. 'See if there's anything I can do.'

'No.' The word came out more sharply than I had intended, and I added more softly, 'I've promised myself an early night.'

'You must be poorly then,' she said with a note of triumph in her voice.

'Not any more,' I told her firmly, 'but I have had a really

busy day with clients in and out. I have a stack of new orders and I intend to knuckle down to get started on them tomorrow, bright and early.'

'Well, if you're sure.'

My mother sounded totally rebuffed, and I instantly regretted being so abrupt with her.

'I'm fine, Mum,' I said far more gently. 'As good as new. Really. You don't need to be worrying about me. Maybe pop in sometime when you have five minutes, just for a cup of tea, but I really don't need checking up on. I'm a big girl now.'

I had barely put the phone down when it rang again and I tutted with exasperation. Then, realizing it might be Chay, I snatched it up, determined to give him a very large piece of my mind. Luckily Martin spoke before I could launch into the tirade of abuse that was primed and ready on the tip of my tongue.

'How are you, darling?' he said sweetly, his deep voice full of very real concern.

'Oh, much better,' I said, a bit too quickly, because the next minute he was offering to come round, bring a take-away and keep me company. 'I wouldn't do that,' I responded, equally quickly, 'just in case you catch whatever I've had. My neighbour has made sure I've had something to eat and I'm planning an early night. Perhaps give it until the end of the week, make sure I'm completely clear? You're far too busy at work to risk contracting a virus that might lay you up for days, Martin.'

I'd said exactly the right thing to discourage a visit any time soon and I tried not to look too closely at my motivation for keeping him away, but eventually I gave into a bit of idle analysis. He had recently become exactly the kind and concerned guy I had always wanted in my life, and I didn't need to remind myself that besides being extremely attractive he was quite a catch. There was obviously nothing wrong with Martin, so what on earth was wrong with me? When had I suddenly become so picky, and why?

Paying him back, perhaps, for his months of quite inconsiderate behaviour? Who would blame me? I knew that really wasn't my style, however, and there must be more to it. Was I distancing myself in case I really was pregnant, or had I already decided that he wasn't exactly what I wanted, after all? I didn't want to think about what – or even who – had brought me to that conclusion.

I couldn't give such disturbing thoughts the attention they deserved. I was too tired and too confused. I couldn't even bother to compare the relatively quiet life I had so recently led to the chaos my life had become in a startlingly short time. Or to remind myself that it wasn't supposed to be like this at my age.

I was making my way wearily up the stairs when the phone rang yet again and I was seriously tempted to ignore it. In the end curiosity got the better of me, though if it turned out to be Chay I knew I didn't have the energy necessary to give him the ear bashing he so richly deserved.

'Mum, are you OK?'

'Of course I am, Meggie.' Shoulders that I hadn't even realized were tense relaxed and then hunched again as I added, 'Why shouldn't I be?' a shade suspiciously, as the thought that Chay might have been on the phone to my daughter as well as to my mother came worryingly into my mind.

'Oh, no reason – except I thought you looked a bit tired over the weekend.' Then she laughed ruefully, 'Small wonder when your daughter turns up with piles of dirty laundry *and* expecting the proverbial fatted calf.'

'I enjoyed having you here,' I told her truthfully, 'and taking care of you again for a little while.'

'Perhaps,' she said, 'but maybe having Dad thrown into the equation was a bit much to expect of you. Though you two do seem to be getting on pretty well.'

'A case of us having to, and being adult about an awkward situation. Obviously we both want to see as much of you as we can when you come home. It's easier for you if we're all together, rather than you running backwards and forwards between the two of us.'

I hoped that making it clear Chay and I were spending time together only for her benefit would disabuse Megan very quickly of any ideas she might have that this was anything more than a convenient arrangement.

'Oh.' I was very much afraid she sounded disappointed, but could well have been imagining things.

'Anyway,' I went on determinedly, 'how are things going? You've all settled into your accommodation, have you, and really are enjoying the course so far?'

Distracted, Megan was eager to say how much they had all enjoyed the shepherd's pie, and would probably be expecting one every time she visited home. She said how keen they were to begin their community placements. She sounded so happy that my own spirits lifted considerably and I went to bed in a much more positive frame of mind.

My mother arrived just when Jean and I had stopped for a mid-morning break and were enjoying a well-deserved cup of coffee. Resigned to a lengthy interruption to my planned work schedule and a probable interrogation, I invited her in.

'This is my friend and neighbour, Jean,' I told her as she paused at the kitchen door, probably surprised to find that her normally unsociable daughter did actually have a friend. 'Jean, this is my mother, Ann.' She was even more surprised, and even a little shocked when Jean's dog, Ben, came trotting in from the garden, gave her an incurious glance and then settled quietly in his basket in the corner.

'A dog,' my mother almost gasped. 'You said you'd never get a dog.'

Jean turned from where she was pouring another cup of coffee and said with a smile, 'Oh, Ben is mine. Tessa very kindly said I could bring him with me when I come to do the cleaning.'

'Well,' my mother said, 'I *thought* I noticed a vast

improvement just as I came through the hallway.' She took the coffee from Jean and looked at her approvingly as she added, 'Housework never was my daughter's forte and this place was looking quite neglected at times.'

'Thank you for pointing that out, Mum. I will allow that I have noticed and appreciated that there is a definite change for the better. However, I must just clarify that Jean isn't a cleaner by trade, though she is obviously very good at it, but she allowed me to persuade her to work for me to our mutual benefit. After a relatively short time I'm already discovering that, besides the house, she also has a real knack with my clients.'

By this time we had settled round the table and my mother was looking at Jean with definite appreciation. 'About time Tess accepted some help,' she told her. 'I must say I'm surprised and pleased. She's always been too independent for her own good.'

'I just wish I had a knack with computers as well,' Jean confided ruefully.

'Computers?'

'I think Jean means that with computer skills she could help with the accounts, too,' I explained. 'You know I'm almost computer illiterate. It's as much as I can do to turn mine on. I lose more than I manage to log on to those damn spreadsheets.'

'You should have asked me,' my mother said, as cool as can be. 'You called me a silver surfer the other day, but I've become quite interested in other aspects of computing. I did a Microsoft Excel workshop ages ago and

I'm perfectly capable of feeding a few figures in. The computer does all the adding and subtracting for you. I did a short accounting course, too, just to keep my brain busy.'

I gaped at my mother and Jean positively beamed. 'I guess we have a third member of the team right here, then?'

'But you're always so busy,' I protested, shocked by the newly acquired skills my mother was apparently gaining while I thought she was taking things quietly.

'I like being busy, Tessa. Like Jean, I would far rather be useful than fritter my time away, it goes too fast anyway when you get to my age. Now,' she looked as if she was metaphorically rolling her sleeves up, 'when would you like me to start?'

Well, this was all too much for me, but I listened to Jean and my mother making plans while the coffee went cold, and then found myself ushered up the stairs to my work area. We all squeezed into the doorway and contemplated the admittedly cluttered room.

'You need more space,' my mother stated emphatically, looking around and shaking her head.

'But this is the biggest bedroom. I don't *have* more space.' Then, thinking I was interpreting the way her thoughts were going correctly, I said flatly, 'I am *not* taking over Meggie's room as well, so you can forget that.'

'I wasn't thinking of Meggie's room.' She looked affronted. 'I do realize she still needs a home to come back to, but what about the garage?'

'What about the garage?' I frowned. 'It's full of stuff and, well, it's *outside*.'

Jean was clearly more on my mum's wavelength than I was, and she was looking quite excited. 'A lot of people turn them into another room – with growing families and the high cost of moving house it's a much cheaper option – and for you it would be ideal.'

I was yet to be convinced. 'Ideal for what?'

'Think about it.' She nodded enthusiastically. 'With the majority of your clients in the more mature age bracket, shall we say, a room on the ground floor will make life easier all round.'

They both stood looking expectantly at me, and I just couldn't let them down. 'It sounds great, in theory, but how much is it going to cost me? Though I've made a steady living, the bit I have put aside might not be enough for these grand plans, especially while I'm subsidizing Megan at university.'

My mother barely waited for me to finish speaking before she chipped in. 'You could get Charles to do the work and I can help out with the cost.'

'No, and no,' I said emphatically.

'Why not?' she said, looking at me as if I was quite mad. 'He would give you a good price for the necessary work and my money is just sitting there. It will be yours eventually, anyway.'

'If we do this, we do it my way, or not at all,' I insisted. 'I love you, both of you, for your enthusiasm and brave offers of support, but we have to think about this properly and not rush into anything. In theory it sounds great, and I would certainly welcome the extra space. Being sensible, however, we need to see if between us we can generate a steady increase in profit, don't we, before we can justify the expense of a scheme like this?'

They acquiesced meekly enough but I had a feeling there would be no stopping them once they got the bit between their teeth. I suddenly felt as if I was part of a pretty formidable team when it had always seemed to be me against the rest of the world. I wasn't entirely sure which I preferred, if I was honest. I had been living in my comfortable rut for a very long time and, the thought of such radical changes scared me half to death.

'Anyway,' my mother said as we went back downstairs, 'you both have work to do. I can't work on the computer in your sewing room without disturbing you, especially if I have to refer to Jean's expertise with accounts from time to time, so I'm going home for my laptop. I'll see you both later.'

'Why don't you stay for a bite to eat first?' Jean offered. 'It'll just be a sandwich and won't take long to prepare.'

'Good idea,' I approved. 'An early lunch would be great because once I get started I won't want to stop again. I need to crack on and earn the pennies to pay for the fantastic improvements you two are busily persuading me are a good idea.'

'You could expand even more sometime in the future.' My mother's enthusiasm suddenly knew no bounds, it seemed. 'You know, open your own showroom.'

Laughing my head off at the way she was already bestowing fashion-designer status on me, I was about to ask her if she could see my designs on the catwalk, when Jean popped her head back out of the fridge from where she was gathering various cold meats and cheeses for sandwich filling and said, 'Probably best you leave that pressed tongue alone in case it was that which was upsetting your stomach.'

'You've been sick?' My mother was on to it immediately. 'You said it was nothing.'

My heart sank. 'It was nothing,' I insisted. 'I'm absolutely fine now.'

'But you have the constitution of an ox, you've never been sick in your life – except. . . .' she didn't continue, in fact she calmly went on making tea, but I knew she had immediately jumped to the same conclusion as Chay had, and I knew she wasn't going to leave it there.

The minute she got me on my own my mother was going to start asking some very searching questions. Like, could I be pregnant and if I was – who on earth was the father?

Over a sandwich that I had trouble forcing down, I calmly joined in with the discussion about various ways in which the business could be improved and the roles that my newly employed assistants would be taking on. We even hammered out proper working hours and reasonable wages, because making the odd outfit suddenly didn't seem nearly enough.

All the time we were talking and appearing to enjoy

181

the food, the company and the plans we were making, I was conscious of my mother's worried gaze returning to my face time after time. I was also well aware it was only Jean's presence that was forcing her to remain silent and that the restaint must have been killing her.

In the end I could linger no longer. I realized that there was no way she would leave the house before she had tackled me with her burning questions. Sure enough, as I made my way up the stairs she was hot on my heels.

'Are you pregnant?' she hissed before we had even reached the top.

'Keep it down, will you?' I scowled over my shoulder, 'Or do you want to take out a full page advertisement in the *Brankstone Echo?'*

'Jean's washing up, she can't hear us above the water running. Why on earth doesn't she use the dishwasher?' she queried inconsequentially, before she suddenly remembered to go back to the far more serious question. 'Well, are you?'

'Of course not,' I stated with far more certainty than I actually felt, and then even more firmly, 'Of course not. Whatever made you ask that?'

'You've been sick,' she pointed out, 'and you never are. The only time I have known you to be sick was when you were pregnant with Megan.'

'Everybody gets a stomach upset sometimes.' I dismissed her suggestion. 'I'm not immune, you know.'

I could almost see the cogs in the wheels of my mother's busy mind slipping into place and hear the clang as the penny dropped. She stepped into the sewing room behind me, and closed the door firmly.

'Is this what Charles was talking about?' she asked, staring at me so hard that her gaze almost burned where it rested on my face. 'Is *he* the father?'

CHAPTER SEVENTEEN

'I am *not* pregnant.'

'Are you sure?' my mother quizzed, looking at me closely, obviously unwilling to just give up and go away. 'Only it seems a bit of a coincidence that Charles should ring me like that. Now I discover you've been ill and kept it from me.'

'I'm sure,' I replied firmly, and that would have been that had not my mother, obviously not entirely convinced, pressed one last time.

'*Are* you?'

Had I only answered in the affirmative, she would have given up, and in my heart I knew it, but suddenly my resolve crumbled and I muttered, 'No, not really.'

She was totally shocked, and absolutely stunned into silence at an answer she really hadn't been expecting, despite her insistent questioning, and then she said, 'Oh, *Tessa*,' and I promptly burst into floods of tears.

I found myself gathered close and shushed like the

child I immediately became in my mother's arms, except that this wasn't something that my mother could make go away.

'How could this happen, Mum?' I wailed. 'I don't know what to do.'

'Well,' she said drily, 'I think we both know how it happened, but,' she patted my shoulder and assured me, 'we will work out what to do between us. I think we both know by this stage in our lives that having a baby isn't the end of the world.'

'But a single mother, at my age.' Not strictly true, an insistent little voice reminded me, but I managed to disregard it. 'A single mother,' I repeated, 'with a grown-up daughter. I could die of embarrassment. How could I have let this happen?' Fresh tears ran down my face and I snatched up a piece of material and buried my face in it, wishing with all my heart that this had never happened.

'What's done is done,' my mother said briskly. 'You can't turn back time, though I'm sure you must be wishing it were otherwise. We need to think about this when we have both calmed down, and consider your options with clear heads.'

I peered at her over the crumpled cloth. 'How can you be so kind to me after I have let you down – *again*?'

'Darling.' She smiled. 'I'm your mother, not your keeper. I don't have to agree, disagree, approve or disapprove of what you choose to do with your life, just be there to support you through good and bad times. I'm doing no more for you than you would do, if the shoe were on the other foot, for Megan. That's what being a parent is about.'

'A pretty lousy one I've turned out to be,' I sniffed, blew my nose and said, 'I don't know what the hell Megan is going to make of this.'

'You're a wonderful mother, and Megan might surprise you. She will certainly support you. Anyway,' she squared her shoulders, 'Jean will be wondering where I've got to. I'll take your accounts books downstairs and she can help me to make head and tail of them.' She picked up the books and gathered together the mound of receipts and invoices that made me shudder every time I looked at them. She had reached the door when she paused, before turning to look back at me. 'The one thing we haven't discussed – yet,' she said, 'is just whose baby this is.' Without waiting for a reply she walked out and closed the door quietly behind her.

I collapsed on to the nearest chair, stared ruefully at the ruined blouse front that I had been mindlessly using for a handkerchief, wondered if there was enough material to cut out another, and wished with all my heart that that particular problem was the worst of my worries.

As ever, I lost myself in the tasks of cutting cloth from the various rolls and swatches of material, before pinning and stitching the shapes that would eventually culminate in a finished garment. Before I knew it, Jean was calling to tell me that supper was ready. It was only then that I become aware of the tea tray she had brought in and placed on the table without my even noticing.

It appeared that my mother had taken the books home with her after going through them with Jean until she felt she had a handle on what exactly was needed.

'Ann seemed thrilled to be involved in what you do and quite excited to be part of your plans for expansion,' Jean confided over the best spaghetti bolognese I had ever tasted. 'She was saying how hard you've worked all your life and made a good living. She's obviously very proud of you.'

But not right at this moment. I didn't have to remind myself that by rushing heedlessly into bed with Chay without giving any heed to the possible consequences I had let us all down. What on earth had I been thinking? I felt my lips curve into a bitter smile as I admitted that the plain truth was, I hadn't been thinking, not at all.

'Leave the dishes, Jean,' I ordered when we had finished. 'You've done more than enough for one day and look at Ben, on his feet and wondering when he's going to get his walk.'

'Oh, will you look at the time?' Jean gasped. 'It will be a quick one for him tonight because I have a t'ai chi class in less than an hour. I wouldn't bother, but I think it's good for me to go.'

'I'll take him,' I offered. 'If you think he will come with me, that is.'

'Are you sure?'

I could tell Jean was tempted, but not liking to take advantage – after all she was doing for me, too.

'I'll enjoy it,' I assured her, and I knew that I would,

especially after being indoors all day. 'I can either bring him back here afterwards, or take him home. You've already told me where you hide your spare key. Let me do something for you, just this once, please?'

Jean laughed, 'Well, when you put it like that ... though you've actually done more for me than you will ever know.' I looked askance at her, and she went on, 'For the first time for years I have something to get up for in the morning and someone who actually appreciates me besides my dog.'

'And you've done much more than help me out here,' I said bluntly, since honesty seemed to be the order of the day, 'I'm learning the meaning of friendship and that I can actually depend on someone besides myself.' I almost said more, since we were being honest, but I saw her glance at her watch, and urged, 'You get yourself off now. Ben and I will be fine.'

In fact, he whined so much after Jean left that I gave up on the idea of tidying the remains of the meal away before walking him and reached for his lead, telling him, 'You win, mate.'

It was quite an experience walking through the park with a dog padding along beside me. It was already getting dark, but the place was surprisingly well lit and well populated, too, with others also out for an evening constitutional accompanied by their four-legged friends.

Almost without exception they took the time to pass a greeting, or at least share a smile. One or two obviously recognized Ben and they paused to ask after Jean, hoping that she wasn't poorly.

'Perhaps I really should be thinking about getting a "Ben" of my own,' I told him and he looked up at me, tongue lolling, and wagged his tail happily. Simple creatures, dogs, I realized; they didn't ask much from life, but gave so much of themselves.

It took a moment or two before it occurred to me that, if my recent fears were realized, far from walking a dog in the park I would instead be pushing a pram. Then what was going to happen to all the grand plans my mother and Jean were persuading me to consider for the business? That was what I wanted to know.

I thought back to the days of Megan's childhood, when I had to fit my dressmaking business around her needs. It had often been a nightmare, trying to keep both her and my customers happy, and she hadn't been a tiny baby when I had left the shelter of my parents' home to realize my dreams of independence. The thought of starting all over again with a young child at my age was, frankly, terrifying.

The mellow mood the walk had put me in, vanished in seconds as I turned into my street. It was just his luck, or lack of it, that found Chay pulling up alongside me in his four by four at that very moment.

'Hello,' he said, in a friendly fashion, just as if we had parted at our last meeting on the best of terms. 'Got yourself a dog, have you?'

'And *what*,' I hissed, glaring at him, completing the sentence over my left shoulder as I marched away, 'has that got to do with *you*?'

He floored the accelerator and drove past me away down the street, and I thought he had gone.

'Good riddance to bad rubbish,' I muttered under my breath, and then watched in exasperation as he parked his vehicle outside my house further along the road and made his way back towards me on foot.

'I thought we should talk,' he said, turning and falling into step beside me.

'About?' I asked abruptly.

'You know what about. This – this situation we find ourselves in.'

'And that situation would be? Oh, yes, don't bother to remind me, the fact that we seem to be making a habit of repeating the same mistakes – even though this time you would have thought we were mature enough to know better.'

'That's a bit harsh.'

'Close enough to the truth to make us both feel pretty uncomfortable though, isn't it? And,' I turned on him and demanded, 'just what the hell do you think you were playing at when you told my mother what was going on?' I turned away and carried on walking with Ben close beside me, through my front gate. I had no problem in ensuring that it swung back on its hinges, effectively blocking his way. A childish action, I knew, but satisfying nevertheless.

'I didn't tell her exactly. . . .' Chay began, pushing the gate open again without a murmur and following me up the garden path.

'Just enough to whet her appetite, arouse her suspicions and start her prying until she got to the truth,' I fumed. I pushed my key into the lock and shooed Ben inside before turning on Chay again. 'Now, I think you've done enough damage for the time being and, basically, I would like you to push off back to wherever you've been, these last – fifteen years or more, isn't it?'

'Look,' he put a hand on my arm, 'I know you're upset.'

I shook his hand off as if his touch burned me. '*Upset*, Chay? Upset doesn't even *begin* to cover how I feel. You have absolutely no bloody idea.'

'Then talk to me – please.'

My first instinct was to tell him where to go again, but something stopped me. Perhaps because he looked as confused as I felt, and perhaps it was my acknowledging at last that I was at least fifty per cent to blame for the predicament we found ourselves in.

'Tea?' he offered, heading for the kitchen. He'd started to fill the kettle even before I replied.

'I don't think that's going to help,' I said drily, 'but go on then.'

I unclipped Ben's lead and he padded across to his bed, turned round twice and flopped down with a sigh.

'He's cute,' Chay said. Cups and saucers chinked as he set them out on to a tray, and he started warming the teapot. 'Rescued, is he?'

'Rescued, yes, but not my dog. I walked him for my friend along the street. Least I could do really.' Suddenly

191

it all poured out, how Jean had been such a wonder, my mother suddenly getting involved, the suggestions they had come up with.

'Well, it all sounds marvellous, Tessa, and no less than you deserve.' Chay sounded genuine in his encouragement. 'With the help you're being offered and, at last, the freedom you need, you can go far and get the rewards you so richly deserve. If there is anything I can do. . . ?'

He was sitting at the other side of the table by this time, pouring tea into the cups, and I stared across at him. 'I think you've done enough, don't you? If I'm to be a single mother again, there is no way I can think of expanding at least for another eighteen years.' I didn't exactly burst into tears but my eyes filled and I had to try very hard not to blink and allow them to fall.

'I'm so sorry.' Chay did look utterly devastated, but I could tell he had to force himself when he said, 'You do have choices.'

'Abortion?' I said flatly, adding, 'You know that I wouldn't do that.'

I thought he looked relieved but was trying very hard to hide it. 'Can I say something?' he asked.

'Say away,' I said encouragingly, 'especially if it's something helpful.'

'Without you biting my head off?'

I was about to deny that I would do any such thing, but even I realized that my track record lately spoke for itself, so I nodded instead.

'This is not history repeating itself. Our circumstances

are very different—' Chay began.

'Like us being married when Megan was born and not married when this one is,' I cut in because I couldn't help it.

'We are,' Chay reminded me, 'because I'm pretty certain that the decree absolute was never issued.'

'But not in any way that matters,' I said bluntly, 'the lack of a decree doesn't change the fact that we've been divorced in every way that matters for years.'

'It may matter to the child eventually,' he pointed out, 'that his or her parents were married when he was conceived.'

'Nobody cares about that any more.'

'I care, and if you're honest, I think that you do too. I can support you both now; you could even be a full-time mum.'

'So,' I kept my temper with difficulty, mindful of the promise I had made, 'I give up my business and all the plans for it that I just shared with you, to raise your child, and you give up – what, exactly?'

'I wasn't saying that you should be a full-time mum, only that you could be, if that's what you chose. When I talk about support I don't just mean money – though lack of it is what probably destroyed us before – I mean in every way. Tess, I know I let you down, badly, all those years ago, but I swear I would never do that to you again.'

'What are you saying exactly? That we pick up the pieces of our marriage where we left off all that time ago and put it back together? Chay, we are virtually strangers. We had a one-night stand, to put it bluntly. You can't build a brand new future on the strength of that – even if we are expecting a baby as a result of it.'

'I think we could at least try,' he said stubbornly.

Exasperated didn't even begin to describe the way I felt. 'You're trying to do it again.'

'What?'

'Turn back time, and I'm telling you that it won't work. Life isn't that simple and too much water has flowed under the bridge. You have a life with Millicent that doesn't include me. You wanted the divorce papers so that you could marry her, remember?'

Chay didn't answer immediately, just stared at me for a very long time. Something made me hold my tongue, then he spoke. 'That,' he said, so quietly that I had to strain to hear him, 'all changed when I found out I was still married to you. Ever since then, turning back time is all I've wanted to do.'

CHAPTER EIGHTEEN

The air between us was electric and the silence deafening, broken only by a gentle snore from the dog curled up in his bed. Then the door opened and Jean walked into the tense atmosphere.

Ben leapt to his feet and bounced around her feet with his tail going fifteen to the dozen. Chay jumped to his feet at the same time.

'Oh, sorry, I didn't realize you had a visitor or I'd have rung the bell,' Jean apologized, bending to scoop the excited Ben up into her arms. 'I didn't want to disturb you if you were working.'

'It's fine,' I said, unable to look at Chay after his extraordinary outburst. I hadn't even had a chance to ask him what on earth he meant and now the chance was gone. 'This is Charles, Megan's father and my ex-husband.'

'Oh.' Jean looked even more confused than I felt, but she quickly gathered her wits about her to say, 'Very pleased to meet you.'

They shook hands and to my relief Chay made his excuses and left pretty swiftly. His cup of tea sat untouched and cooling rapidly on the table.

Jean looked at it and grimaced. 'Was it something I said?' she asked.

'Not at all. He'd said what he'd come to say,' I assured her and then, changing the subject abruptly, I asked her, 'How was your class?'

'It probably is doing me good, but I can never practise when I get home, as we're supposed to do, because I can't remember any of the moves and positions.' She laughed and pointed to the teapot. 'If that's still hot I'd love a cup and then I must get myself home to bed.'

We sipped our tea companionably and I was oh, so tempted, to spill the whole sorry tale, to share some of the responsibility for my own stupid actions with the wonderfully capable Jean, if only to see what she would make of it. In the end, though, I just couldn't do it. I valued her good opinion of me too much to see the shock and disappointment on her face.

She, after all, had stuck to what sounded like a very difficult husband through thick and thin, following the vows she had taken when they married to the letter up until the day he had died. She hadn't just thrown in the towel when the going got tough.

I would have to confess not only to giving up on my marriage probably far too easily, but then to being too careless to ensure my own divorce was finalized, adding a final *pièce de résistance* by having a fling with the very man I had never quite got around to divorcing, and then compounding the whole thing by finding myself pregnant as a result. Even I had difficulty believing my own absolute stupidity.

I suddenly felt Jean's hand covering my own and heard her say, 'Tessa, you look as if you have the cares of the world on your shoulders. Is there anything I can do to help?'

I found myself looking up into her kind eyes, and her comment and simple question was my undoing. I felt the tears trickle down my face and said sadly, 'There is nothing anyone can do to help, Jean, but if I thought there was I would tell you.'

Of course, she wouldn't give up that easily, first concentrating on pouring both of us more tea, finding me a box of tissues, and then insisting, 'A problem shared is a problem halved.'

I shook my head, 'This one isn't going to go away.'

'Are you ill?'

I shook my head again.

'Is it us?'

I stared at her, 'Us?'

'Your mother and me, getting carried away with these dreams of aiding you in expanding your business and putting you under pressure to make changes you might not be ready to make.' She looked at me anxiously. 'After all, you were managing perfectly well without our interference.'

I managed a watery smile. 'The way I'm feeling has nothing to do with that, I promise you, though I think I might have sabotaged those plans.'

I knew I would tell her, that I had to. Jean had become a dear friend even after so short a time and I knew in my heart that she would have sensible advice to offer regarding the situation I found myself in if anyone did.

'You don't have to tell me anything right now, Tess, I can see that you're struggling and my piling on the pressure isn't going to help. I'm your friend and I'm sure you know I will always be here for you. When you're ready to talk I will listen.'

She stood up, carried the tray of tea things over to the sink, and I knew I couldn't let her leave without first confiding in her. I had even opened my mouth and began, 'Jean, I'm. . . .' when the doorbell rang.

We stared at each other and it was Jean who said, 'Now, who on earth can that be at this time of night?'

I smiled at her comment, 'It's only about 9.30, Jean, not midnight. I'd better go and see, hadn't I?' I moved towards the door as the bell pealed out again, a short sharp, impatient ring.

'Do you want me to stay, or shall I slip out through the back door with Ben?' Jean offered.

'Stay, please. I'll get rid of whoever it is as quickly as I can.' I hurried out into the hall as the bell rang yet again.

For a moment I didn't grasp the identity of the woman standing on my doorstep, because it was the last place I would expect to find her. She took full advantage of my confusion.

'You and I, Tessa Wallis, need to have a few words.' With that she pushed past me and marched towards the kitchen – the only room with a light on.

'Just who the hell do you think you are, barging into my house?' I demanded, slamming the front door shut and hurrying after her.

'Who's this?' The woman indicated Jean who was standing against the sink with Ben in her arms. 'This is a private matter. Tell her to leave.'

'None of your business, and she stays.'

I straightened my shoulders and glared, taking in the appearance of this interloper. Tall, with chin length glossy black hair, a meticulously made-up face, even at that time of night, Millicent was carrying a real grudge against me for some reason, if I was any judge.

'What do you want, Millicent?' I demanded sharply, adding for Jean's benefit, 'This is Cha – my ex-husband's girlfriend.'

'Ex-husband's *ex*-girlfriend, if you have anything to do with it,' Millicent said nastily. 'Just what the bloody hell do you think you're playing at?'

I had a horrible feeling I knew what she was talking about. It would appear that my mother wasn't the only one Chay had been blabbing to. I wondered why he didn't just take out a double-page advertisement in the *Sun* and have done with it.

'I have absolutely no idea what you're talking about,' I

said as firmly as I knew how, praying that I sounded convincing and determined to give nothing away.

'No, of course you don't,' Millicent sneered nastily. 'First, apparently, there's some sort of a hitch with the divorce – and that was hard enough to swallow after God knows how many years of separation – now you're claiming to be *pregnant* with Charlie's baby.'

She looked outraged, as well she might, I had to admit. I would be outraged if I was in her very high-heeled shoes. She ploughed on, obviously equally determined to have her say. 'What was it, Tessa? An immaculate conception, because it's impossible to conceive by email or telephone to my certain knowledge, and that's all the contact there has been between you and Charlie for years. I know for a fact that you and Charlie can barely stand to be in the same room together. I don't know what – exactly – your little game is, but I tell you now that it will not work. Charlie is mine and we are going to be married whether you like it or not.'

'Good for you,' I applauded cheerily. 'Congratulations, Millicent, and I can assure you, you are very welcome to him, because I certainly don't want him.'

Still in full flow, it took a minute or two for Millicent to realize what I had just said. The stream of vitriolic words stuttered to a halt and she stared at me, dark eyes narrowed in clear disbelief.

'So you say,' she sneered eventually. 'So why all the far-fetched excuses?'

Suddenly I was weary beyond belief and just wanted

this woman out of my house and out of my life – along with Chay. Allowing him back into my life had been a huge mistake and, looking at the trouble it had caused, one that wouldn't be repeated, not even for Megan's sake.

'I don't have to explain myself to you,' I said, drawing myself up to my full height. 'If you have questions you had better take them to Charlie.'

'But. . . .' Millicent began.

'You heard what she said,' Jean spoke for the first time, and at the tone of her voice Ben bared his teeth and emitted a low growl.

'I'm going.' Millicent tossed her head, and turned towards the door, 'but you can be certain I will be back unless you sort out this bloody mess and release Charlie from this sham of a marriage. Pregnant?' she turned back to look me up and down in the most disparaging way. 'Don't make me laugh. Charlie has *me*, so why on earth would he want to crawl back into *your* bed?'

The front door was slammed so hard behind her as she left that it rattled.

'Well,' said Jean, obviously shaken, 'what a nasty piece of work. She evidently dislikes you, but to invent a pack of lies like that to try and shift the blame for whatever ails her relationship with Charlie on to you is beyond belief.'

'Erm,' was all I could find to say and I hung my head.

'It's not *true*, is it?' she exclaimed. Then interpreting my silence correctly, she added, 'What, *all* of it?'

'I'll make a cup of tea, shall I? Unless you fancy

201

something stronger – you might just need it.'

'Best stick to tea, I think,' Jean said drily with a nod at my stomach. 'I'll get the biscuits out, shall I?'

By the time the whole sorry story was fully told, we had drunk the teapot dry – twice – and emptied the biscuit barrel. At last we sat back and just looked at each other.

I'd expected to find myself a sobbing wreck by this time, but my eyes were dry, probably because Jean just listened and made the odd, non-judgemental comment. She looked neither shocked nor disgusted, just plain concerned.

'So,' she said after some moments, 'you *think* you might still be married, you *think* you might be pregnant, but you don't actually *know* anything for sure, do you?'

'No,' I agreed, 'I don't, do I? What an idiot.'

'Just doing what most of us do in times of crisis and trying your best to ignore it all, hoping it will either go away or sort itself out. I'm right, aren't I? I've done my share of the same over the years. I might have tackled the difficulties in my marriage or even walked away from them. Instead I just let the unhappy years roll by, hoping that the problems would somehow resolve themselves or simply go away.'

'But I really admired you for staying with your husband instead of giving up, like me.'

'Well, I don't know all the ins and outs of your marriage, but I knew I had made a mistake almost as soon as the ring was placed on my finger. Gerald was a cold man married to a passionate woman, and once the initial attraction wore off we very quickly discovered we had absolutely nothing in common. I knew he would be terribly humiliated if I left him, so I stayed, and undoubtedly made us both very unhappy by doing so.'

'That's really sad.'

'But at least it's over, and they say that what doesn't kill us makes us stronger – or something like that. Did Charlie leave you for that woman?'

The question was as sudden as it was unexpected and I answered immediately, 'Oh, no. We married for love – we were head over heels – but were far too young to cope with the reality or the bills and we struggled to keep a roof over our heads. Bringing a baby into the equation was madness, much as we both loved her, and in the end we had to admit defeat. I went home to my parents with Megan, Charlie refused to join us and just seemed to give up totally on our relationship.'

'He didn't support you?' Jean queried.

'Financially, he did,' I explained, but I heard the bitterness creep into my tone as I added, 'but he went to work abroad for several years. It was as if he couldn't get far enough away and from then on our only contact was regarding Megan. It has been that way until very recently. I can't fault him as a father; he saw Meagan regularly even when he was overseas, but thinking we could be friends after all this time was a mistake I won't be making again. Look where it's got me.'

'You won't be the first or the last couple with history between them to end up in bed,' Jean said flatly. 'It's

happened and now we have to look at how we deal with
the current situation.'

'What do you suggest?'

'Perhaps start by looking at the possibility that you *are*
actually pregnant and that you *are* still married. I know
it probably doesn't matter that much in this day and age,
but the baby will be Megan's brother or sister, and born
from the same marriage, if that is the case. Would you
really want this child to know it was born as a result of a
one-night stand?'

'Plenty probably are,' I pointed out.

'Undoubtedly, but not many from mothers in their
forties is my guess.'

'Point taken,' I agreed ruefully.

'So when did you do your last pregnancy test?' Jean
asked. If I had felt stupid before, I really felt like a
complete idiot when I had to confess, 'I haven't actually
done one.'

'You. . . ?' Jean looked at me as if I were completely
mad.

'Isn't it a bit soon?' I queried.

'Oh, no. These days they give a result very early on and
they are extremely reliable, too.' She sounded very
knowledgeable, but she explained, casually, 'I pick up all
kinds of facts from newspapers and magazines and even
from listening to gossip on the bus. You'd be amazed what
I overhear. So,' she added briskly, 'there is a late-night
chemist down the road. It just might still be open.'

I didn't know whether to be pleased or sorry when we

pulled up outside a shop that was still brightly lit. In fact I was absolutely scared to death to be facing at last the fact that I wasn't going to be able to ignore the truth for very much longer.

'I'll go in, shall I?' Jean offered. 'After all, there's no chance anyone is going to think it's for me.'

I tittered nervously. 'Would you mind?'

She was back within minutes waving a paper bag aloft, and minutes after that we were back safely indoors.

'Off you go.' Jean ushered me towards the stairs. 'No time like the present. I'll go and put the kettle on.'

She looked up expectantly from pouring tea as I walked into the kitchen on legs that had real trouble supporting me and fell limply into the chair opposite.

'Well?' she said, as I sat in silence. 'I think I know what the answer is, because you look as if you've seen a ghost.'

'I. . . .' I began hesitantly, struggling to get the words out, 'I'm *not* pregnant,' and then I burst into tears and cried as if my heart would break.

CHAPTER NINETEEN

'I have no idea why I'm crying,' I sobbed, as we viewed no fewer than four different brands of pregnancy test, the full contents of the paper bag that Jean had brought away from the pharmacy, all of which confirmed that I definitely wasn't carrying a child. 'I never wanted a baby.'

I had been convinced, so convinced, that I was pregnant that somehow, despite its being the very last thing that I wanted I felt bereft – as if something precious had been taken from me, which was absolutely ridiculous.

Jean poured more tea, it was obvious that she just didn't know what else to do.

'I didn't,' I said again, as if she had queried my statement.

'Of course not,' she said eventually when my sobs had subsided to an occasional hiccup, 'but you would have loved it anyway.'

I knew she was right and I felt a surge of grief for the

child I had truly believed I was carrying. I wondered when the far more sensible feeling of relief that I had been expecting was going to kick in.

'I suppose I had better let Chay know it was all a false alarm,' I mused out loud.

'Chay?' Jean looked confused.

'My ex-husband,' I explained. 'His name is Charles but I've always called him Chay. Everyone has nicknames at school – which is where we met and fell in love. At least he and Millicent can get on and book the wedding now.'

'Not if you're still married,' she pointed out.

'Oh, yes, I'd forgotten about that.' I pulled a face.

'Look, it's really very late now, and you have a full client list in the morning. It's been an emotional few hours and I suggest we shelve all of this for now. You say you've looked for the decree absolute, but you don't actually recall ever receiving it. Given the fact that the firm of solicitors you used has, apparently, disappeared off the face of the earth, I think we can safely assume that the final decree doesn't exist. Tomorrow we'll have a look at what can be done in a case like this.'

'Do you think there are other cases like this?'

'I'm sure there are,' Jean said comfortably. 'People lead such busy lives that it's quite easy for paperwork to be overlooked. The whys and wherefores aren't important, only what happens next.'

I hugged her as she left and stood on my doorstep until I saw her go safely in through her front door, then I closed my own and leaned back against it with a gusty sigh.

As I made my way wearily to bed, I contemplated the way my life seemed to be lurching from one drama to the next, starting – I had to say – with Megan uttering the words: *Dad said to tell you he'd like to have a word with you*. It all seemed so very long ago now but, in truth, it was no time at all. It had probably happened just around the time I had been contemplating how quiet my life was going to be when my daughter left home.

I never thought I would say it, but I hadn't actually had the chance to miss Megan very much at all. I wondered if I was supposed to be grateful for that, fell into bed and was asleep in seconds. I only woke when I heard Jean letting herself in through the front door the next morning, and I barely had time for a slice of toast before my first customer arrived. There was no time to think at all, which I found was just how I liked it – thinking hadn't been a lot of help, thus far, I realized.

I had a cup of coffee with Jean and my mother mid-morning, and they stated their intention to take themselves off to Staples, having dismissed my office supplies as 'totally inadequate'. My mother had professed herself 'relieved' when she heard that I was not pregnant after all, though I felt sure her expression showed a different sentiment. What that sentiment was, exactly, I wasn't entirely sure, since she couldn't possibly be disappointed.

When I came down looking for a lunchtime sandwich they were still missing, but in the centre of the kitchen table – was my mother's laptop, switched on and logged on to the Internet with the Google logo beckoning.

I was actually trembling as I sat down and pulled it towards me, fiddling with the little pad that moved the cursor until I had a feel for it, then I typed into the box, 'I have a decree nisi – what must I do next?' and all these items of information popped up. I even found a site that allowed you to type in an exact scenario and there I found ones being discussed that bore a distinct resemblance to mine. It seemed I wasn't the only person who had overlooked the fact that they were still legally married – but didn't want to be.

Someone had written, very helpfully, that they understood a decree nisi never actually ran out of time, but after more than twelve months had elapsed you could not apply for a decree absolute without explaining your reasons for the delay, probably to a judge. Until you had the decree absolute, someone confirmed, you were definitely still married in the eyes of the law.

A little more searching provided me with a phone number that I could call to obtain free legal advice. If I'd known this was going to be so easy I could have started sorting it out the minute I'd realized there was a problem instead of wasting time searching for obsolete law firms and non-existent paperwork. I was making a note of the number when I heard a key turn in the front door and I was standing at the worktop making sandwiches by the time my mother and Jean walked into the kitchen.

Ben had been sleeping peacefully in his basket all this

time, I barely knew he was there, but he was up out of his bed and dancing around Jean as he always did the minute she appeared.

'Must be great to be loved so unconditionally,' I commented, placing the plate of sandwiches on the table and encouraging them both to, 'Tuck in.'

'Actually, about Ben,' Jean said hesitantly. 'I wondered if I might ask you a favour.'

'Ask away,' I said persuasively, 'I must owe you a million by now.'

'I've asked Jean to come along to the computer classes with me. She's very keen but doesn't like leaving Ben for too long, as you know,' my mother put in, 'and it's tonight.'

'I realize it's very short notice,' Jean apologized, 'and I will quite understand if it's not convenient.'

This from the friend who had sat with me until the early hours – drying my tears and calming my fears – showing me how to gain control of my life again, instead of letting it control me.

'Why wouldn't it be convenient, Jean? He's no trouble at all. If all dogs were like Ben I would have one myself tomorrow. Why don't we all have a meal together here later and then I can walk him so that you don't have to rush.'

By the time we'd finished eating the sandwiches I had admired the items purchased to supplement my meagre stationery supplies and insisted on reimbursing the pair of them, Win Etteridge and her sister Madge were already beating an eager path to my door.

210

The change in Madge was astounding. The astonishing thing was that the transformation had been achieved with not much more than a decent haircut. Gone was the limp and lifeless grey hair that had previously hung around a face that could only be termed dour. She hadn't followed her sister's example and gone for a trendy look, but with a much shorter, layered style, together with the smile on her face she looked years younger. I was certain I could even detect a dab of pink lipstick and, of course, she was wearing an outfit of a style that suited – and fitted – her, because it was one of mine.

'My, don't you look a picture,' I said and was rewarded with a beaming smile.

Instead of taking a back seat, this time she vied with Win for my attention. She had her own, very definite ideas of what might suit her.

'I'm beginning to regret forcing her to come along,' Win said, with a satisfied smile that belied her words.

The whole of the afternoon was devoted to these two clients, and the financial rewards, though undeniable, were not foremost in my mind because the job satisfaction from the sisters' pleasure was a reward in itself.

Everyone, even my mother, got involved in each stage of the proceedings, from the choices made regarding material and style, to the fittings of garments in the final stages. I had never seen my mother so animated.

'I had no idea,' she said, when the sisters eventually left, 'just how much was involved in what you do: the effort you put in to making sure that each customer gets exactly what they wanted, while guiding them away from choosing anything totally unsuitable. I'm very proud of you and so pleased to be involved in such a satisfying process.'

'Marvellous to feel useful, isn't it, Ann?' said Jean.

'Well,' I said, blinking the silly tears that threatened, 'I feel I could achieve anything with you two behind me. We'll talk more about those plans we were discussing when we have more time.'

'Cold meat and salad?' Jean spoke from the depths of the fridge. 'I think that's about all we have time for.'

'With some of that crusty bread we brought back with us this morning,' my mother chipped in, bustling over to the bread bin.

After they had left and I had cleared away the remains of the meal I was pleased to get out into the fresh air. It was already dusk but the park was bustling with other dog walkers, and again the majority of them greeted me as if I was one of them. As I walked home I kept expecting Chay to pull up alongside me again and I wasn't sure whether to be relieved or disappointed when that didn't happen.

I still couldn't think what he had meant by the comment he had made before we were interrupted by the untimely arrival of Jean. What had he been thinking, to say he wished he could turn back time? Did he mean he wished we were still married in more than name? That he wished we had never been married? Or simply that he wished the divorce had gone through when it should have done?

I wasn't surprised by the ring of the doorbell, I knew Chay and I had unfinished business. The fact there was no baby would put a whole new slant on things, as would my discovery that the divorce could apparently go through without much of a hitch. Chay would then be free to pick up his life where he had left it off before he had felt obliged to offer his support to me.

Flowers filled the doorway, and I had already opened my mouth to admonish Chay for his extravagance and to ask him what on earth they were in aid of, when they were lowered to reveal Martin wearing a very nice suit and an apologetic expression.

'I hope you don't mind me calling in, darling,' he said smoothly, 'but I couldn't stay away a moment longer. How are you feeling?'

With everything that had gone on I had all but forgotten my 'illness', but I recovered my wits quickly to say 'Oh, much better, thank you.'

'Oh, I am pleased.' Martin handed over the gigantic bouquet and looked at me expectantly. He was quite obviously waiting for me to invite him in. Since I'd already told him I was better I felt I had no choice.

Opening the door wider, I told him, 'You'd better come in. Come through to the kitchen while I put these in water. They are beautiful. Thank you.'

I was chatting away as I bustled around finding a vase and suddenly realized that Martin wasn't answering. I turned to find him standing in the doorway with a look of pure horror on his face.

'What. . . ?' I began, and following his gaze saw that he was staring at Ben who was sitting quietly in his bed looking right back at him.

'It's a *dog*,' he said, as if the gentle little mongrel was a rabid monster of some kind.

'So it is,' I agreed. 'He is actually quite harmless. His name is Ben, and I'm minding him for my neighbour.'

'Well, thank goodness for that,' he said quite sharply. 'I thought for a minute he was yours.'

I felt quite stung by his tone, and his assumption that any decision I might make about getting a dog should have anything to do with him, but I let it go and watched him perch on a chair as far away from the dog as he could get. It would have been funny if it weren't so annoying.

'So what brings you here, braving any lingering germs?' I asked, feeling obliged to go and put the kettle on, and adding over my shoulder, 'What can I get you – tea or coffee?'

'I actually brought champagne,' he said. Startled, I turned round in time to see him placing the bottle he must have been holding behind his back on the table. 'It came straight from the fridge, so it is nicely chilled.'

'Are we celebrating something?' I said turning back to reach into the cupboard to get glasses down.

'I hope so.'

I hadn't heard him get up from the table, but Martin's

voice very close to my ear made me jump. I whirled round to face him. At the same time he dropped suddenly on to one knee, took my hand in his and said, 'Will you marry me, Tessa?'

CHAPTER TWENTY

To say I was shocked by this totally unexpected turn of events was the understatement of the century. I said the first thing that came into my mind. 'Oh, Martin, this is so sudden, I don't know what to say.'

It sounded like a line from a sloppily written soap opera and I had to fight the urge to giggle, except I could tell from his expression that Martin was deadly serious. Not only that, but he was clearly waiting for an answer, and by his smile he wasn't expecting it to be, 'No'.

'You must know how I feel about you, darling.'

'Well, no,' I felt obliged to say honestly, 'I've never actually had any idea about your feelings for me and that's why your proposal of marriage has come as such a shock. We've hardly had what you would call a serious relationship, have we? In fact, at times it has been casual to say the least. We've actually spent very little time together for all that we have known each other for quite some time. I don't even have your telephone number.'

He had the grace to look slightly uncomfortable at something that could only be seen as a statement of the truth. Perhaps realizing that he looked a bit foolish now it was becoming obvious he wasn't going to get the immediate answer he had evidently been expecting, Martin scrambled to his feet.

'I may not have been as attentive as I could have been in the past,' he admitted, taking both of my hands into his, 'but that's because I had to be sure of my feelings before making a commitment.

'You must admit that I've made a real effort to change recently. It's taken me a long time to reach this decision because I wanted to be certain it was the right one. I know now that with you by my side there is nothing I cannot achieve. The way you reacted to the cancelled weekend in such an understanding way only confirmed that. My efforts at that time played a big part in setting the business back on its feet and have resulted in my being offered a partnership.

'If you do me the honour of becoming my wife I can promise you the kind of life you can only ever have dreamed of, a life where money is no object. You know where I live and have a good idea of how I live, and things can only get better. I just know that you will fit right into my world.'

'But what about my world?' I heard myself saying.

Martin looked at me oddly as if he wasn't sure he had heard me correctly. 'Well, I've just said that I will take you away from all this.'

'Away from my home and my family?'

'I wouldn't dream of stopping you from seeing your daughter and your mother, Tessa, but Megan is at university now, an adult with a life of her own, just as your mother has hers and, once we're married, I will be your family, surely?'

'And my business?'

'Darling.' He laughed. 'Of course I won't be expecting you to *work* for a living. What would people think? My salary will be more than enough to keep us in comfort. Apart from attending the odd function or charity event, when I will be more than proud to have you on my arm, your time will be your own. I have every confidence that you will fit right in to the circles I move in.'

I was sitting at the kitchen table with the open champagne bottle and a full glass in front of me when my mother and Jean walked in. Jean's attention was taken up with the devoted Ben dancing round her legs but my mother stared at the bottle and then at me.

'Something to celebrate?' she queried.

I met her look with a straight one of my own and told her, 'Martin has asked me to marry him. Will you drink a glass of champagne with me – and you, too, Jean?'

Jean looked bemused, but fetched glasses from the cupboard, saying, 'Just a sip for me.'

Both women accepted a drink but it was noticeable that no one raised a glass for a toast.

'Are you sure you know what you're doing?' my mother

asked, after taking a reluctant sip that looked as if it might choke her.

'Oh, yes,' I said, 'I do know exactly what I'm doing. He said I would never have to work another day in my life, you know.'

'Oh,' the two women said in unison.

Their faces mirrored the same look of complete dismay, and though neither said a word I knew they were each seeing the collapse of the tentative plans for my business that we had so recently discussed with such enthusiasm. They were also each accepting that this was my life and my decision; it was only that that was keeping them from commenting.

I reached for my glass, intending to raise it and to make a toast of my own, but at that precise moment the doorbell went.

'It's a bit late for visitors, isn't it?' my mother said with a frown.

'I'll get it, shall I?' Jean said, automatically slipping into her daytime role of greeting my customers at the door and she was gone before I could reply.

'It's your. . . .' she began when she came back in, followed by Chay, then, clearly flummoxed, she left it to him to finish her sentence, which he did with the one word, 'husband'. Then he continued, 'There are things that need to be said, Tessa, and as far as I'm concerned there is no time like the present.'

'We'll take Ben for that walk now, shall we, Jean?' my mother said, with a meaningful nod towards the door when Jean looked as if she might demur – which was hardly surprising because it was quite dark out and they both knew very well that I would have already walked the dog while they were out.

'Champagne?' I lifted the depleted bottle and waggled it in Chay's direction as soon as the door had closed behind them. 'You'll find a glass in that cupboard over there.'

He fetched a glass without a word, watching silently as I filled it, then he asked quietly, 'What are we celebrating?'

'A proposal.' I smiled up at him. 'A marriage proposal. Martin has asked me to marry him.'

Chay's face went very pale and then very red. He looked as taken aback as if I had slapped him. 'You can't,' he stated flatly.

I set my jaw, and told him, in no uncertain terms, 'I think you will find that I can do whatever the hell I like, actually.'

He sat down, leaned forward across the table and demanded, 'Does he know about the baby?'

'That's just it, Chay.' I took a huge swallow of champagne, which made me choke a bit. I hoped he would think that the tears in my eyes were from trying to catch my breath. 'I discovered late last night that there is no baby. There probably never was. So you see, we're both free to get on with our lives.'

He looked shocked, stunned, but recovered very quickly. 'And is that what you want? Is *he* what you want.'

'Well, he is quite a catch.' I tried to be flippant.

'What can he give you that I can't?'

'I wasn't aware that I was being given a choice,' I said, aware of the hammering of my heart as I wondered just exactly where this was leading, 'but I've been offered a life of luxury and leisure with money no object. Can you match that?'

'Ha!' The sound of Chay's laughter was harsh, 'you would be bored to tears inside of a week.' He dismissed this notion emphatically. 'He obviously doesn't know you very well at all.'

'And you do?' I challenged. 'What do you know about me after fifteen or more years with precious little contact, a recent one-night stand and an oversight with legal paperwork that means we aren't *quite* divorced?'

'I know that you are the only mother I could ever have chosen for my only child, I know that you are fiercely independent and brave and strong. I know you don't suffer fools gladly and that's why you have always despised me for walking away all those years ago when the going got tough, but no more than I have always despised myself. You were little more than a child but like an adult you stepped up to the mark and took on the sole responsibility for bringing up our child.'

'I had my parents' support.' I heard myself defending him, without really knowing why, because he was right – I had despised him for leaving.

'You should have had mine.' His tone was anguished. 'You were my wife and Megan was my child. I thought,' he hesitated, and then rushed on, 'when you said you were pregnant I thought I was being given another chance, an opportunity to put the past right.'

'Stop it,' I told him fiercely, then in a softer tone, 'Stop it. You must realize that however much you wish it, Chay, you can't undo the past or change it in any way. Resurrecting our marriage in a probably well-intentioned but quite futile effort to correct mistakes of the past wouldn't work, for either of us. We've already proved we didn't have to be in a relationship together to be good parents – you only have to look at Megan. If I had been pregnant I know very well you would have been a loving, supportive father to the baby – just as you always have been to our daughter.'

'Thank you. It means a lot to me to hear you say that.'

'I've been angry with you for too long and you've been carrying the burden of guilt for just as long. It's time now for us to let the past go and move on, to accept that we both made mistakes, starting with marrying far too young and for all the wrong reasons. Staying married for equally wrong reasons isn't an option either of us should be considering.'

'I agree,' Chay said, and looked as if he might have said more if the phone hadn't started to ring.

I almost didn't pick it up, but then I was glad I had. 'Megan,' I said, sharing a smile with Chay. 'I have your dad right here and we were just talking about you. It's late for you to be ringing, sweetheart. What's so important that it couldn't wait for the morning?'

*

'There she is,' I turned to my mother. 'There's Megan coming in now with Chay. I told you she would make it on time.'

My mother adjusted the hat she had insisted upon wearing. 'Well, it is a big day for her,' she said with a smile, 'will you look at that child, at how alike they are.'

We watched the toddler with his coppery curls determinedly make his way towards her on sturdy legs and reaching out his arms to be lifted. Laughing, Megan scooped him up and spun him around without a thought for the gown she wore as the little boy shrieked in delight.

A hush had begun to descend, people were taking their places. The ceremony was about to begin.

'Come here, trouble,' Tom said, lifting his son from Megan's arms, 'and if you are very good you shall see your Mummy get a very special prize for being a fabulous student and graduating with a first-class honours degree in midwifery – and all while she was gaining some first-hand experience having you.'

Nothing like learning that you are about to become a grandparent to make you focus on what really matters and remind you, quite forcefully, what being a family means. However, I think Chay and I had both already realized, almost from the moment we discovered we were still married, that we wanted it to stay that way. It had taken that telephone call from Megan to make us forget our stupid pride and simply admit it.

223

ACKNOWLEDGEMENTS

My thanks go, as always, to all at Robert Hale Ltd, especially Gill Jackson, Amanda Keats, Ruby Bamber, Erica Holmes-Attivor, Nick Chaytor, Catherine Williams and David Young.

I am blessed every day to have the love and support of my lovely family, my children, Shane, Kelly, Scott, not forgetting Mike and Jess and my gorgeous grandchildren, Abbie, Emma, Tyler, Bailey and our newest addition, Mia.

Not forgetting my stepchildren, Rachel, Debbie and Mark, my sisters, Barb and Pat, and the colleagues I worked with for so long in the HSC Admissions Office at Bournemouth University, Pam M, Kate H, Sarah, Kate T, Jill, Jane, Gail, Angela, Alison, Lukasz, who will remain dear friends.

www.pamfudge.co.uk